Corporation's First Annual

SAUSAGE FESTIVAL

A Novel

Garry Ryan

Pages Press...

LIBRARY AND ARCHIVES CANADA CATALOGUING IN PUBLICATION

RYAN, GARRY 1953-
CORPORATION'S FIRST ANNUAL SAUSAGE FESTIVAL/GARRY RYAN

ISSUED IN PRINT AND ELECTRONIC FORMATS. ISBN 978-
I. TITLE

EDITOR: JEREMY SHANNON
COVER IMAGE: ELISE MULLEN
AUTHOR PHOTO: LUKE TOWERS
BOOK DESIGN: RICHARD YOUNG

PRINTED IN THE USA

Pages...
Books on Kensington - 403-283-6655
New - Used - Bargain

1135 KENSINGTON RD. NW
CALGARY AB T2N 3P4
403-283-6655
WWW.PAGESKENSINGTON.COM

"Be good to the kids,

they'll be around a hell of a lot longer than you."

H.U. Ryan

For

my family

ONE

<u>Tuesday, May 6</u>

0

When *did freedom become freedumb?* Garrett thought as he read the Krotch brothers' editorial in the Upper Canada Press (UCP).

His phone rang. He reached for it, pressing green. "Hello?"

Jacolynne asked, "How's it goin' dad?"

"Good. Ella's asleep." *It would be great if she could sleep for a little longer.*

"What's the matter?"

"Just reading the paper. The Krotch brothers are whining because their guns were removed from one of their houses during the flood. Some people lost their lives, many lost their homes, and all the Krotch boys can talk about is their guns. Now they're going to sue the RCMP for doing their jobs."

"I heard they fired a news anchor for mispronouncing their name."

"They get real upset when Krotch doesn't rhyme with coach."

"Didn't that anchor end up in Corporation?"

Garrett heard a whimper from the spare bedroom of his fourth floor condo. "Yep."

"Okay if I pick up Ella around five?"

"Sure."

"Gotta go."

"Bye." He went to the spare bedroom. Blonde haired, blue eyed, round-faced Ella stood in her crib, blinking at the light coming through the open door. She wore a white sleeper adorned with strawberries. There was a decided ordure about her. He inhaled, picked her up, using his right hand to touch her bottom where he felt that unmistakable gooey consistency. Closer inspection on the changing table revealed this was a neon green from the navel, down, around, and up the mid-back kind of disaster. Holding her at arms length, he took her to the tub. She smiled as he peeled off the sleeper and diaper, running the water, and using the showerhead to rinse away the emerald tattoo. *I can't remember David or Jacolynne having neon poop*, he thought while the last bits swirled around the drain. He plugged the tub then dropped the diaper and sleeper in a plastic-lined garbage can.

Ella splashed the water. He handed her a rubber dolphin and she began studying the flukes as water rose up to cover her ankles. Garrett washed his hands at the sink while watching her in the mirror. He didn't bother to dry them as he turned, grabbing a bar of soap, kneeling, dipping the bar in the water, lathering it up in his hands, then washing her arms and back. As soon as he finished, his phone chirped. He leaned back, drying his hands, pulling the phone from his shirt pocket, and reading a text from David. "You there?"

Garrett kept one eye on Ella as he typed. "Yes."

His phone rang ten seconds later. He put it on speaker. David asked, "Dad?"

"We're here. Ella's in the tub."

"She lied to me, Dad." David's voice was fingertips-against-a-food-grater raw with emotion.

"Where are you?"

"In my class. I'm on a break. She lied to me. She went on that spring break trip to Mexico with another guy."

Garrett looked at himself in the mirror, seeing Ella in the background. "Melissa?"

"Yes. I told her how I felt about her. I would have done anything for her."

"You broke up?"

David's voice cracked. There was sobbing. Ella splashed. Garrett turned. Water spattered the front of his pants. Ella lifted her arms, her butt squeaking against the tub bottom, she leaned back, her feet went up, and her head slipped under water.

Thirty minutes later, Garrett backed into the door at Fatima's Salon. He held a tray with two coffees, two breakfast sandwiches, and a strawberry banana smoothie in his right hand while maneuvering Ella's stroller with his left.

The door swung closed. The ceiling was white, the walls red, the chairs black, and mirrors strategically placed to provide the illusion of spaciousness. He swung the stroller around, seeing red-headed Fatima in a white blouse and painted on red cigarette pants with her arms crossed. Not for the first time wondering what Fatima saw in him; a balding, round-faced, white-bearded gopher impersonator. She spoke with a man wielding a full head of back-combed salt and pepper hair. His eyes were a light blue. Michelangelo could have carved his face. He wore a weathered black leather jacket, open-necked white shirt, black jeans, and black leather boots.

Marco, Garrett thought, looking over his shoulder at the door then down at Ella who sensed the tension. The toddler focused on Fatima who was pointing a red fingernail at Marco. "What exactly do you want?"

He put his hands on his hips. "She's my daughter, and I want to spend time with her." Marco turned, spotting Garrett. "We're kind of busy right now." He lifted his right hand, glancing at the blue-faced Yacht Master Rolex on his wrist. "Come back in ten minutes."

"I don't think so." *Oh shit.* Garrett set the drinks and sandwiches on the counter.

Marco smiled at Fatima, turning to Garrett. "Get out of here."

A pair of hair clippers hummed.

Marco moved toward Garrett who stepped sideways and away from Ella. Marco was an inch shorter than Garrett but a decade younger. Marco leaned his head to the right. "You're that old fart. The one who looks like a gopher and used to be Dayna's teacher. Now you think you can move in on my family?"

Garrett nodded, *Just keep your mouth shut.* "Yep. I'm that old fart."

Marco moved within a metre of Garrett, sticking his index finger in between Garrett's man boobs. There was the raw stink of second hand garlic on the younger man's breath. Contempt lit Marco's eyes as he surveyed the manscape. "You've let yourself go man. I don't want you in my daughter's life. So you take the brat in the stroller–" He pointed at Ella. "–and get the fuck out of here."

Garrett took a breath. Flashing back to this morning's horror, he thought, *There's more shit coming out of this guy's mouth than Ella's butt.*

Marco opened his mouth, stepping closer, then his head snapped back. Fatima had the fingers of her left hand hooked in the back of Marco's mane. She used her right hand and the clippers to cut a swath from forehead to crown.

Marco reached to stop her. Garrett grabbed Marco's right hand, ducking when the left swung for his temple. The cuff of Marco's jacket scuffed the top of Garrett's head.

Fatima pushed Marco forward. She tucked her left toe in front of his ankles. He tripped, falling into the door. It swung open. He rolled onto the sidewalk. Tufts of black hair stuck to the soles of his leather boots. His ex-wife pointed the clippers at him. "You want more?"

Marco propped himself up with elbows. There was an unfinished stretch of stubble highway running through the hair plugs in the middle of his scalp. He put his hand up, feeling the patch. "What did you do to my hair?"

"It'll grow back."

He said, "Dayna's twenty. You can't keep her from seeing me."

Fatima held the door open, kicking at his feet. "You're right. Dayna can make up her own mind." She pointed the clippers at her chest. "I've already made up mine." The door closed. She set the clippers down, bending over, picking up Ella who nestled comfortably in one arm, tucking her knees English saddle style around Fatima's waist. The toddler took a strand of Fatima's red hair in her hand. They touched noses. "Laura wants to be our wedding planner."

Garrett shook his head. "Laura?"

Fatima turned to him, studying him with violet eyes. "We made a deal. She'll stay on her meds for a full year. She's been on that new medication for a month now. It's made a big difference."

He looked at Ella who was watching him as well, waiting for an answer. *How come I get the feeling that you understand far more than everyone else thinks you do?* "Being a wedding planner's a very stressful job."

Fatima sat down on the black faux leather couch, reaching for her coffee. "It is." Ella pointed at her stroller then squeezed a fist.

He grabbed the bag under the stroller, lifting a bottle of milk, handing it to Ella. The cushion sighed as he sat down next to them. "How much is she charging?"

Fatima watched Ella as she leaned back, took the rubber

nipple, and began to drink. "Nothing. It's a gift."

Garrett took a sip from his mocaccino. "Are we going to talk about Marco?"

"He's back in Calgary. He says his buddies need his wheeling and dealing talents here. Anyway, that's the story he's telling. It's become convenient for him to reconnect with his daughter." She rested her chin on Ella's head. "I worry about Dayna being hurt. I've wasted enough time on Marco."

"David's just been hurt by Melissa."

"What happened?"

"I guess she went on that trip to Mexico with another guy."

"Harrah alikum."

Ella said, "Fit on her!"

Fatima looked at Ella then looked at Garrett. "Who taught her how to swear in Arabic?"

. . . .

YYC News

<u>Corporation Mayor Evades Drug Trafficking Question</u>

by Gwen Chorny

When asked about his alleged connection with drug trafficking, Mayor Rodney Richardson said, "I believe the Krotch brothers are in the right. The RCMP had no business removing firearms from their home. The flood was just an excuse."

Richardson made the statement on Monday outside the Corporation town offices. When asked about a video connecting him to drug trafficking in central Alberta, he ignored the question and instead used the opportunity to support the Krotch brothers.

In a related story, one of Richardson's long time associates, Milo Ferguson, was accused of uttering threats. Ferguson allegedly threatened to drop a resident of Corporation in a tailing pond if he did not hand over copies of a video showing Richardson bragging about his alleged drug enterprise.

RCMP Constable Raye Lennox from the Corporation detachment added, "There is an ongoing investigation into the allegations. If and when sufficient evidence is gathered to justify an arrest, the media will be notified."

· · · · · · · · · · · · · ·

David sat at his father's kitchen table. His metallic white motorcycle helmet perched like a loyal canine companion on the chair next to him. His black hair and red beard were trimmed short. David's grey eyes stared out the window where a poplar tree's limbs shivered in the wind. "She blamed me for the whole thing."

Garrett looked at the grey paint on the walls of his condo. Then he looked at the maple cabinets and blue pearl granite. *Why the hell did this have to happen to David? I thought after Marie, we'd be done with this.* Then the anger began to simmer. *Melissa, do you have any idea of the kind of damage you've done?*

"She said it was my fault."

Garrett focused on his son. "Bullshit."

David looked away from the window and at his father. "What?"

"She is full of bullshit. She was lying and cheating and she got caught."

"What?"

Garrett got up from the oak chair, moving to the fridge. "Don't let her bullshit you."

"But I love her."

He opened the fridge door. "She's not going to change. The bullshit is not going to stop whether you love her or not. It's who she is." Garrett took a jug of milk from the fridge, setting it next to the espresso machine. "I'm gonna make us a coffee. We're going to have a cup then get our shit together."

"Why do you have to get it together?"

"Marco's back in town."

"Marco? You mean Dayna's dad?"

Garrett nodded as he took two cups out from the cabinet, setting them next to the machine.

"You'd better call Jacolynne and tell her. Dayna's gonna need someone to talk with."

Garrett leaned his back against the counter while the machine heated up. "Melissa's a liar and a cheat. Marco is a deadbeat dad. They are responsible for their bullshit, not you and me. We're both gonna have to deal with those truths." He pointed at his chest. "It hurts today. Tomorrow it'll hurt a little less."

TWO

<u>Wednesday, May 7</u>

0

YYC News

<u>Mayor Denies Video Evidence</u>

YYC News has acquired a copy of an incriminating video of Corporation's Mayor Rodney Richardson. The video shows Richardson with his pants down around his ankles while being fellated by a calf.

When asked about the video, Mayor Richardson said, "If you show that video I'll sue you. It's an obvious fake."

Richardson was then asked if he'd seen the video. He replied, "How could I? It doesn't exist. It's fake news."

The mayor is an outspoken supporter of the Krotch brothers, Canada's wealthiest siblings, and majority share holders of Nova Bank and several media outlets. The Krotch brothers were unavailable for comment on the video.

THREE

Thursday, May 8

0

Garrett and Fatima sat at the table in his kitchen. He'd prepared a Greek salad for supper. Fatima put her fork down, picked up the wine glass, and sipped. He drank ice water. She set the wine glass down. "Marco took Dayna and Siobhan to the Flames game."

He looked at the white gold engagement ring on her finger. "It's game seven of the semi-finals."

"Box seats. The girls are pretty excited."

Fatima's cell phone rang as Garrett poured her a second glass of wine. She set the glass on the coffee table then walked over to her red leather celebration-of-spring purse on the kitchen counter. She reached inside, pressing her thumb on the face of the phone, walking back to the couch, tapping answer and speaker.

"Mom?" Dayna asked.

Garrett heard the hurt in Dayna voice and leaned forward. The leather cushion groaned. *What's happened?* He looked up at Fatima, seeing the fear in her violet eyes.

"Can you pick us up?" There was weeping in the background.

"Who's crying?" Fatima looked at Garrett, shaking her

head.

"Siobhan."

"What's happened?" Fatima set her glass down.

Garrett stood, pulling his keys out of his pocket. "Where do we pick you up?"

"Sunnyside station. We're on the C-Train."

Fatima followed Garrett to the door. "On our way. Are you safe?"

"Yes. We'll explain when you get here." Dayna ended the conversation.

Garrett grabbed his phone, following Fatima out the door, down the hallway, then down the stairs to the car park. His blue Ford was parked next to a pillar. Fatima climbed in the passenger seat, shaking her head, closing the door, and hauling the seat belt across her body.

Seven minutes of silence passed as they crossed Fourteenth Street and waited at the lights on Tenth. He tapped the steering wheel until the light turned green and he could turn north. He turned right at the Safeway next to Sunnyside station. Three LRT cars whispered up the hill. In the foreground Dayna and Siobhan sat on a bench under a yellow sign saying LOOK BOTH WAYS FOR TRAINS. Red haired, violet-eyed Dayna wore a red Flames jacket, matching Siobhan's whose black hair fell down the front of her face. She leaned against Dayna who had her hand on the girl's cheek. Both had just turned twenty–their birthdays a week apart. They'd met a year ago when Siobhan apprenticed with Fatima as a hairdresser.

Garrett parked the wrong way on the one-way street, waiting while Dayna helped Siobhan to her feet. They squeezed into the back, up against Ella's car seat. He turned into the Safeway parking lot as Fatima twisted in her seat to face her daughter. "What happened?"

Garrett watched the girls in the rear view mirror. Siobhan

wiped her eyes with the tissue Fatima handed her. The girl's face was framed by her black hair and accentuated by hazel eyes. Her jaw was angular, her lips full. When she and Dayna walked down the street, accidents had been known to occur. David had nicknamed them the fender benders.

Fatima looked at Garrett's reflection. "Marco had a few drinks then he told Siobhan he loved Eurasian chicks and asked Siobhan to join him in the bathroom."

Garrett glanced at Siobhan who exhaled slowly, nodding her head.

Dayna said, "Siobhan tried to laugh it off, but he didn't take the hint then put his hand on her thigh. She pushed it away, and I told him to stop being a pig."

Siobhan said, "Then he got mad and said he was just having a little fun with his girls."

Dayna leaned her head back, staring at the grey fabric roof of the car. "I stood up and said we were leaving."

Siobhan wiped her nose. "He got angry when Dayna took my hand and he called us dykes."

Dayna watched Garrett as he turned in his seat, then she said, "I told him he had no right to judge us. That it was my business who I love."

Siobhan looked out the window. "Then he told us to get the fuck out."

Fatima leaned against her door, watching Garrett.

He asked, "Are you hungry?"

"What?" Fatima raised her eyebrows. A pair of parallel worry lines crossed her forehead.

Dayna asked, "What do you mean?"

Garrett tried to smile. "This is a coming out. We should celebrate."

"Mom? How come Marco was wearing one of those knit beanies?"

Fatima glanced at Garrett then said, "He was getting in-"

she pointed at her fiancé "–this one's face so I got him with the clippers."

"Now I'm really pissed off." Dayna's face turned red to match her mother's blouse. "Marco comes back into my life, gets drunk, disowns me, and tries to hurt Garrett." She leaned forward, touching Garrett's shoulder. "What were you saying about dinner?"

FOUR

<u>Friday, May 9</u>

0

Upper Canada Press
<u>Social Media Goes Too Far</u>

The reputation of another Canadian patriot is being dragged through the sewers of social media. A grainy image of a person resembling the Mayor of Corporation, Alberta has been widely viewed, raising a number of serious questions.

The first question is how is it possible that an unverified video can be used to besmirch an individual's character? Yet that is exactly what has happened. So-called comedians in the United States have used this unverified video to pillory Rodney Richardson.

The second question is why the people behind the video are able to post it without revealing their identities? Isn't everyone in our society entitled to face his or her accusers?

Finally, all Canadians should be worried about the dangerous precedent of this new approach to public shaming. All of us are vulnerable to unscrupulous, cowardly, and malicious attacks such as this illegal posting of a video of a person purported to be the Mayor of Corporation, a man of unparalleled good character and selfless service to the public.

• • • • • • • • • • • • • • •

"That's kind of odd." Dayna pointed at a black pickup truck stopped in front of them at the lights. It had NO MERCY in chrome across the tailgate and a black pair of salsola bull balls dangling from the trailer hitch. The box of the truck was filled with pink gladiolas and purple lavender. The driver's shaved head was a bobblehead above the blooms.

Dayna and Siobahn sat in the back of Garrett's car, Fatima sat next to him as they drove north along Shaganappi Trail. Calgary's Nose Hill Park was on their right. The prairie grass greened in the light rain. The grey blue belly of the clouds blocked a faraway view of the Rockies.

Fatima looked out her window. "Great to see rain."

Dayna leaned forward, touching her mom's shoulder. "What are you worried about?"

Fatima turned to Garrett. She tried to open her mouth to talk but tears came instead.

Garrett looked in the rear view mirror to see a glance exchanged between Siobhan and Dayna. He recognized fear. *It's not about rejection.* "She's worried how the world will treat the two of you."

"What the hell does that mean?" Dayna sat back against the seat, crossing her arms. Siobhan put her hand on her lover's shoulder.

"It means she's your mother, she wants to protect you, and she worries about you. That's what it's like to be a parent. You always worry about your kids and what will happen to them." Garrett looked at Fatima, recognizing fire behind the tears. She nodded. He glanced at the traffic behind. *Should I pull over?*

Siobhan said, "Your Mom's on our side. Garrett's on our side. It's obvious."

Dayna leaned into Siobhan.

Garrett said, "Siobhan said it best."

Dayna nodded, wiping her eyes with her sleeve. "You're worried about people like Marco?"

Garrett nodded. Fatima began a fresh round of weeping.

They arrived at Shazia's, red eyed and weary from weeping. The restaurant was at the northern edge of the ever-expanding city in a strip mall, next to a dance studio. SUVs and mini-vans dropped off and picked up dancers in pink tights and tutus.

Garrett parked next to a grey mini glacier, an icy remnant of the snow plowed from the parking lot over the winter.

Inside Shazia's, a young woman with black hair wore a black blouse and slacks. She asked, "Have you got a reservation?"

Garrett looked over the counter, smiling, and pointing. "We're right over there." Jacolynne waved a free hand from the far side of a table while grappling a squirming Ella. Her husband Mark stood next to her at over six feet with his green eyes and black hair. Garrett followed the women as they walked across the restaurant. Jacolynne smiled, stood, hugging Dayna, Siobhan, and Fatima in turn. Mark took Ella in one arm while dispensing hugs with the other. Garrett glanced at the big bellied, cross-legged, bronzed statue atop the hefty table between the windows.

"A special family celebration?" Heads turned to face Shazia who ran the place and often worked tables. She stood six feet, wore black slacks, a white blouse, and a smile touching her eyes.

Garrett pointed at Siobhan and Dayna. "This dinner honours them."

Shazia nodded, tucking a wayward strand of black hair behind her ear. "Would you like drinks or are you ready to order some appetizers? The samosas are especially tasty today."

Jacolynne nodded. "I'm starved. Could we start with some

of those?"

"A selection of veggie, chicken, and beef?" Shazia looked at Ella who hid her face against Jacolynne's neck.

"Sounds goo–" Fatima began as her voice cracked. She covered her mouth and coughed. "I've got a frog in my throat."

"Ribbit."

Everyone at the table turned to stare at Ella who smiled, enjoying the attention. "Ribbit!"

Garrett grinned as the laughter jumped from Dayna to Siobhan, becoming a prairie whirlwind of delightful relief whipping around the table.

David arrived a minute later. He went around sharing hugs before squeezing in beside his niece. "How's my Ella?"

The main courses arrived about fifteen minutes later. Garrett cut off a morsel of coconut squid, looking around the table while he chewed. Ella sat on David's lap, driving a tablespoon into a bowl of rice. David's face was thinner, revealing a loss of at least twenty pounds. He tucked his cheek next to Ella's, helping her guide the spoon into her mouth. Garrett thought, *It took me a while to learn when people like Melissa betray you it makes you weak in the short term. But it makes you exponentially stronger in the future. I just hope David won't take as long as I did to discover the truth of it.*

Fatima chewed a mouth full of curried lamb, leaning into him, and pointing her fork. She covered her mouth. "What are you thinking about?"

Garrett looked at her, then around the table, seeing the expectant faces of his family listening in. Except of course for Ella who scooped up more rice from David's plate. "I was just wondering how I got to be lucky enough to be part of this family."

Ella's voice stopped conversation when she sprayed rice. "Me too!" She swung her spoon up, accidentally whacking David on the end of his nose. He laughed through tears.

After dinner, Garrett and Fatima watched their family climb into David's Jeep and Jacolynne and Mark's SUV as they headed off to a movie. Fatima stood next to him with her left hand holding his. Her head rested against his shoulder. He inhaled her lilac perfume. She said, "Thank you for this."

"For what?" He looked across the lot as Shazia slammed the rear door of a white Escalade.

A fifty-year-old bull of a man with a blonde brush cut and gym-toned biceps leaned out the driver's window. "We'll be back on Tuesday for the first installment." The engine raced. Shazia walked across the parking lot without looking back. Her eyes were black with rage. She stepped past Fatima and Garrett, opening the door, disappearing inside the restaurant.

The Escalade pulled out.

Garrett asked, "What's that about?"

The Escalade turned in front of them. Its wide tires scuffed the pavement.

The passenger looked to be forty or forty-five. His brown hair was tied back in a ponytail. His nose was cocked to one side from an old break. He studied Shazia while reaching down to close his window before turning to the driver. "Why Tuesday?"

The driver said, "Pete, you know we've got a meet with Rod in Corporation on Monday."

Pete's window closed.

Fatima pulled Garrett toward his car. "Insurance."

"What do you mean?" He followed her.

"They're Angels. It's called insurance, but really it's extortion."

"How do you know this?"

"They're old friends of Marco."

Garrett stopped. A mother in a minivan sped past them with a pair of tots in tutus in the back seat. "Marco's a Hells Angel?"

FIVE

<u>Sunday, May 11</u>

0

"I'd better get home. Dayna said she would be back by four and I want to make sure she's okay." Fatima put her feet into her red pumps. "See you tomorrow?" Garrett nodded. She kissed him on the lips before going out the door. He watched her walk down the hallway then onto the elevator.

He looked out the window at the traffic on Kensington Road. A man pushed a red baby carriage with spoke wheels filled with garbage bags stuffed with cans and bottles. A woman and a five-year-old in a pink raincoat walked past. Someone pounded on the door to his condo. He turned, walking toward the door. *I hope Dayna's okay.* He opened the door. Marco faced him. He wore a red knitted beanie, black leather jacket, T-shirt, and jeans. *You must have been waiting outside until Fatima left.* Marco used the palm of his right hand against Garrett's chest to shove him back inside. The door slammed shut. Marco said, "You turned my daughter gay!" He pointed his finger at Garrett's nose. "You're gonna stay away from her from now on."

Garrett grabbed the offending finger with his right hand, bending it back. *What the hell do I do now?*

Marco's eyes opened wide then rolled back white, similar

in shade to his complexion. Garrett let go of the finger to grab hold of a collapsing Marco then set him on the couch. The leather cushions sighed. Marco leaned his head back, blinking at the ceiling. His eyes focused, looking at Garrett who took a step in reverse. Marco said, "I've got hyperalgesia man! Don't ever do that again!" He went to stand, tried to shake away a head spin, sat back down, put his head in his hands, talking to the hardwood floor. "My buddies are Angels. They listen to me. They're gonna come visit you on Tuesday. You'd better do what I tell you or they will rearrange your face." Marco stood up, making for the door, turning as he grabbed the doorknob. "Nobody fucks with my family." Marco opened the door and left.

Garrett made sure the deadbolt was engaged before going over to the window, looking toward the river. *If I call Fatima about this she'll be upset, and she's already worried about Dayna.* He walked over to his computer, checking the definition of hyperalgesia.

27

SIX

<u>Monday, May 12</u>

O

Melvin Gartner parked the Buick on a patch of gravel behind his barbershop. It fronted onto the paved main street of Corporation. He turned the engine off, got out, and walked to the back door of the shop. He waited for a moment as he turned to look at the sky. Grey blue clouds threatened rain while the east wind kept pushing them against the Rockies. The key in his right hand opened the back door as it had done every Monday to Saturday for the last twenty-five years. He ducked inside, closing the door, walking across the black and white tile to the light switches. The fluorescent lights blinked. He closed his eyes for a moment while their glare bounced off the mirrors onto the walls to his left and right. He inhaled the scents of floor cleaner, machine oil, and hair products. Even though he'd always worked alone, there were a pair of 1924 Hercules hydraulic barber chairs. His friend Riley had helped him restore them to their glory days of shining black leather, white porcelain pedestals, and gold highlights. He got busy putting on a pot of coffee and turning the CLOSED sign to OPEN.

The coffee pot spluttered as he looked in the mirror. His black hair was cut short and combed. There was some grey at the edges. His round face was clean-shaven, his white shirt ironed, and there was a sharp crease in his grey slacks. For a moment he saw his gaunt reflection repeated as it curved off into infinity in the mirrors on opposing walls. The phone rang. He recognized the number of his sister-in-law, Louise, in Calgary, feeling his heart pounding. "Did you find him?"

There was a pause at the other end followed by a sob. He leaned against the wall. There was a photo above the phone of him, wife Cathy, and son Derek on a beach at a Cancun resort. Derek was fourteen and standing between his parents. The past smiled back at him, and he saw his son before the anorexia, the rotted teeth – the exquisite hell of a meth addiction.

"Melvin? You there?"

Melvin recognized the voice of his brother-in-law, Dave, who worked for an oil and gas company. "Yes."

"The police just stopped by the house. They found a body with ID on it. They think it's Derek."

Melvin looked at the polish on the toes of his black shoes. "What happened?"

"They say he was stabbed. Cathy and Louise are going with me to identify the body. I'm sorry."

"Can you call me when you get back?"

"You'll be at the shop?"

Melvin nodded. "Yes." He felt a numbness overtaking him when he hung up the phone. An inability to come, go, leave, breathe, or make even the most insignificant decision. The bell above the front door chimed. Rodney Richardson stepped in for his Monday morning trim and shave. Richardson wore a navy blue sports jacket and pants, white shirt, and python skin cowboy boots. His black hair was slicked back. His chin was pronounced, what some would call a lantern jaw. Melvin recalled the time-share salesmen who pursued them while in Mexico. All had slicked back black hair, wore white shirts and blue slacks. They smiled the way Richardson was smiling right now. The glare of perfectly whitened teeth, the calculating brown eyes never getting the memo when the mayor was smiling. The glass in the door rattled against its frame. He sat, propping his boots on the ornamental metal footrest.

Melvin watched his arms and hands as if they were attached to someone else. He automatically took the black cape, draping it over Rod's torso and knees, using the Velcro to snug it around the mayor's neck. Melvin asked, "What will it be today?"

"Just a quick clean up and a shave. Got some business associates coming into town."

Melvin took his comb and scissors off the counter, snipping to even out the cut. Then he reached for the clippers.

Rod's smart phone chirped. He pulled it out, reading a message. Melvin saw it was from Milo.

Derek's dead.

Rod tapped a reply on his phone. "Gotta hurry it up there Melvin. I've a meeting to get to." The phone whispered when its message sent. Rod put the phone in his pocket.

Melvin turned on the clippers, beginning to trim Rod's neck. *My son is dead.* He was just finishing the neck and right ear when Milo's dark grey Ford Expedition pulled up, parking within three metres of the shop window. Milo was at the wheel, just visible behind the tinted glass. His blond hair bobbed to a tune Melvin couldn't hear.

Constable Thorpe's words came back to Melvin. "You know it was Milo who got Derek hooked. He came to the lake the night the kids had their grad. Started handing out pills for free. Can't get anyone who'll be a witness. More than one told me what happened on the condition of anonymity. Will you testify?"

"Shit! Melvin, what the hell you doin'?" Rod leaned forward then stood. He reached up, touching the lobe of his left ear. He turned the fingertips so Melvin could see the smudge of blood.

Melvin turned off the clippers, looking outside. Milo had the Expedition's window open. He was talking to Melvin's nephews Gordon and Terry. They nodded as Milo leaned out, smiling. The boys waved, turning to walk north toward the school. Terry stopped, putting his face up against the glass, waving at his uncle.

Rod used a tissue to dab at his ear. "Get your shit together Melvin."

He tossed the cape at the chair, heading outside into the sunshine. He climbed up and into the Expedition. It backed up, the engine revving, wheezing black diesel smoke from an oversized tail pipe.

Melvin looked at the clippers then set them in their cradle. He took the keys out of his pocket, walking to the front door, locking it, turning the CLOSED sign so it faced out. He walked to the back of the store, using another key to unlock the padlock on the storage room door. *Derek is dead.* A sob ripped through him. His forehead leaned against the door while he concentrated on the lock. It clicked open. He hung the padlock on the loop of the metal hasp and pulled a string to turn on the light. His Remington shotgun and a box of shells were in the corner. The gun had been stored here ever since Derek had become addicted and their house had turned into a junky version of hell. Melvin took the gun in his right hand and the shells in his left. He walked back into the shop, setting the shells on the leather seat of one chair, opening the box, sliding red cylinders into the loading port.

· · · · · · · · · · · · · · · ·

Garrett pushed Ella on the swing in the Hillhurst park near his condo. The sky was prairie blue, the temperature in the mid teens. It felt as if summer might actually arrive. There were even a few buds showing up on adventurous shrubs. Ella laughed as she reached the top of the arc. "Quack!"

He waited for her to come back to him, grabbing the bucket of her swing seat, running underneath. Her laughter was pure, rich music. He turned, looking back at her blonde hair tucked inside the hood of her purple polar fleece jacket.

His phone began to play a tango, vibrating in his shirt pocket. "It's time to go. We're meeting Fatima."

"Tima!" Ella shouted.

Garrett smiled. *What am I going to say to Fatima about Marco's threat and his Angel friends? There's no point in hiding stuff from her. She knows when I'm holding back.*

. . . .

Melvin drove with the shotgun's butt on the floor matt, its barrel leaning against the passenger door of his Buick. He stopped at the edge of the gravel road leading to Richardson's white Quonset hut. It sat at one corner of a section of land. It was a kilometer away in a valley. On either side of the road leading to the Quonset, the fallow field was grey and gold with straw. There were three vehicles parked out front of the Quonset: Milo's grey Expedition, a white Escalade, and a red Dodge Ram pickup truck with a black fiberglass cap over the box. Melvin looked at the ditch. It was half full from spring run off. He grabbed his cell phone from the passenger seat and dialed. It connected, ringing three times before a woman said, "Corporation RCMP detachment."

"This is Melvin Gartner."

"Oh hello Melvin. It's me, Betty. How's Cathy?"

"Grieving."

"What do you mean?"

"Derek was killed in Calgary."

"Melvin, I don't know what to..."

"Betty, I wanted to phone and warn you that a drug deal

is going down at the Richardson place south of town. You know where the white Quonset is? Tell Thorpe I'm there now waiting for him. Betty, I'm hearing gunfire." He pressed end, dropping the phone, shifting the Buick into drive, pressing his right foot down. The engine responded with a roar. He watched the speedometer climb to eighty, holding it there. He looked out his side mirror, seeing the dust boiling behind his car. The breeze caught the horizontal column, rolling it into the ditch. The Buick rattled over a cattle guard. The men in the yard turned toward him. He took his foot off the accelerator, coasting over the grass across from the Quonset, swinging the wheel to the left, hitting the brakes. The car slid sideways toward the three vehicles parked near the open overhead door of the Quonset. Melvin saw two men who were loading plastic wrapped packages into the back of the Dodge pickup.

The Buick stopped about ten metres from the Expedition. It was parked to the right of the Dodge with the white Escalade in between.

Melvin shoved the transmission into park with his right hand, opening the door with his left, grabbing the forestock of the Remington. He stepped out, looking over the hood.

Rod stepped out from the shade in the mouth of the Quonset. "What the hell you doing here Melvin?"

Melvin's peripheral vision caught movement on his right side. He turned to spot Milo coming around the front of his Expedition. He had an automatic rifle in his hands. He swung the gun in Melvin's direction. Melvin lifted his shotgun, pumping in a round.

Milo fired from the hip. The rounds punched the side of the Buick. The barrel of the weapon lifted. Milo fought the recoil.

Melvin aimed at Milo and fired. The blast caught Milo in the chest.

Melvin swung his shotgun to the left, chambering another round. He spotted a man with a ponytail stepping out of the Escalade. Someone said, "Look out Pete!"

Melvin shot Pete in the throat. He dropped to his knees. The Escalade's back door was spattered with blood.

Melvin fired twice more before dropping behind the Buick's front end to reload.

· · · · · · · · · · · · · · ·

Constable Sydney Knox drove a four-door Ford pickup along a stretch of paved two-lane highway ten kilometers south of Corporation. The sky was three hundred and sixty degrees of blue. She pulled at the side of her bulletproof vest. *They don't make these damned things big enough for me. I should have had that breast reduction after the kids finished with the boob.* She looked in the mirror to check the lines at the corners of her eyes, brushing a wayward strand of brown hair behind her right ear. The radio squawked and Bill Thorpe, her commanding officer, said, "I need you for backup Knockers. What's your location?"

Knox thought, *Asshole,* then said, "Ten kilometres south of Corporation."

"Meet me at Richardson's place at the south side. We have a report of a drug deal and gunshots. Arrive silent."

"On my way." She checked the time. *Should be there in less than five minutes.*

"No stops for makeup application."

Knox clicked the button of the mic, pressing her right foot down by way of reply.

Four minutes later she crested the hill looking down on Richardson's Quonset. There were vehicles in the yard besides Thorpe's blue and white cruiser. His driver's door was open. She checked her speed, dropping to sixty before rumbling over the cattle guard.

Something snapped a hole in the windshield just under the

rear view mirror. Knox ducked to her right. A series of stars stitched their way across the glass. It felt like a fist slammed her chest. She swung the wheel to the left. The Ford dove into the ditch, up the other side, through a barbed wire fence, and into the fallow field. The engine warning light flashed as the power steering failed. She braked, stopping, opening the door, falling out the far side of the truck, crawling forward. She lay on her back gasping for air, back against the front wheel, reaching for her Smith & Wesson. With her left hand she wiped her eyes. There was blood on her sleeve. The door alarm bonged. She wiped her left palm on her pants, chambering a round in her nine millimetre. *Breathe! Get the fucker!* There was a burst of gunfire rattling against the Ford's body panels and pinging off the engine block. The door alarm quit.

That's better. One deep, aching breath. *Listen! Forget the pain. Breathe.* She heard the muffled approach of footsteps crackling over the stubble and soft soil. *He's coming from your right.* Knox leaned left onto her hand, got her feet underneath her, leaning her back against the tire. She cupped her left hand under her right, cradling the Smith and Wesson. Her sleeve wiped the blood from her forehead.

"Knockers? That you?" The footsteps came closer.

Another deep breath to steady her hands and her aim.

"Knockers?" This time there was sarcasm in the male's tone.

There was a metallic sound.

He's changing magazines! She rose up to face Rodney Richardson across the hood of the Ford.

"Knoc..." His mouth was an O. He had a black assault rifle in his right hand. A fresh clip in his left. He moved to bring the two together.

Knox aimed, fired once. The bullet took out Richardson's front teeth. She aimed again. The handgun snapped out another round. This one disappeared into Rod's right eye.

The spent shell was a broken tooth jammed in the ejection port. She saw life departing Richardson's remaining eye as it lost focus. He fell sideways.

· · · · · · · · · · · · · · ·

Fatima held a sleeping Ella on her lap as she sipped her coffee. Garrett sat next to her on the couch in her salon. He admired the red walls and the new mirrors. *Fatima is an artist.*

"What aren't you telling me?" Fatima kept her voice low. There was a familiar don't give me any bullshit tone.

"Marco came by after you left last night. He told me he was going to get his biker friends after me because I turned Dayna gay. He wants me out of your lives."

Fatima's violet eyes turned on him. Her anger was fire singeing him.

Shit! Why did I have to tell her?

The fact that she kept her voice low did nothing to mask the rage behind the words. "Why didn't you call me right away?"

Garrett shrugged. "You had enough on your plate. Dayna just came out. I didn't want you to worry. He said he has hyperalgesia."

Fatima shook her head, leaning forward, setting her coffee on the table, and pointing a white tipped fingernail at him. "Don't you ever do that!"

He held his hands out with palms facing the ceiling, his eyes meeting hers.

"Don't you ever try to shield me from his bullshit! That son of a bitch has no right!" Her hand shook like her voice. "What the hell is hyperalgesia anyway?"

"Sensitivity to pain." Garrett's phone beeped. He looked at it on the coffee table. The CBC logo preceded a one-sentence message. **Eight confirmed dead after mass shooting in Corporation, Alberta.**

"It's bullshit. He doesn't have hyperalgesia. He's lying."

. . . .

YYC News
Mayor Amongst Victims in Corporation Shooting

Rodney Richardson, Corporation's controversial mayor is reportedly among the dead following an early morning gun battle. Corporation is located about one hundred kilometres north and west of Calgary. The violence also claimed the life of at least one RCMP officer. Early reports indicate eight bodies were discovered at the scene.

RCMP investigators confirmed the shootings took place on Richardson's property located at the southern outskirts of Corporation.

Corporation has approximately fifty five hundred residents. Billionaires Kristopher and Harold Krotch own properties on Corporation Lake. In recent years, Mayor Richardson and the Krotch brothers have been outspoken supporters of the rights of gun owners.

More details will follow as they are made available.

. . . .

Garrett picked up the phone, leaning his back against the countertop. Jacolynne sat at the kitchen table, attempting to eat a Caesar salad while Ella sat in her high chair, picking up green quartered grapes one by one. Each morsel had to be studied from various angles before being popped into her mouth.

He dialed the number of his cousin, Riley, who lived on a farm outside of Corporation. "Hello?" came after three rings.

"Hey Riley it's Garrett."

"Hello there. Been a while." There was both country and fatigue in his voice.

"I heard about what happened and we wanted to make sure you and Sam are okay."

There was a short pause. "We're okay. Just shook up. It all happened a few kilometers from here. I was outside in my shop. I heard the gunfire."

"How about Sam?"

"He was in town picking up a few things. He's pretty upset. Melvin was a friend of ours."

"Not Melvin the barber?"

"Yep. He and his wife Cathy have been going through some tough times."

Remember, Riley's talking about small town secrets. This could take a while. He waited.

"Family problems."

"Oh?"

Riley said, "Their son Derek had a meth addiction."

"Shit."

"Exactly. Everyone knew Milo Ferguson got Derek hooked on the stuff. Something set Melvin off, because his car is still out at the Richardson place. Word is he heard about his son's death and just snapped."

"Milo is one of Richardson's men?"

Riley said, "Yep. Now the RCMP have got the place all blocked off. Nobody in or out. Apparently one officer was taken to hospital. Nobody's saying how she is."

"She?"

"Her name is Sydney Knox. She's been here about six months. Her and her husband have two little boys. He takes care of the kids. Does computer work out of the house. People around here were just getting to like her." Riley covered the phone. There was a rustling sound.

"We just wanted to know you two are okay, and to let you know if you need anything..."

"Thanks. I'll let you know. I gotta go. Sam is pretty upset.

Melvin was a good guy."

"I understand."

Riley said, "Give me a day or two, and I'll call you back." He hung up.

Jacolynne looked at her father. "How are they?"

. . . .

Sydney Knox sat up in bed at the Corporation hospital. The walls were beige, the floor was grey, and the sun shone through the first floor window. She closed her eyes, leaning her head back, replaying the events just before and just after the shootings. The arrivals of other units, the ride in the ambulance, body count, bodies identitified. The information was coming in gradually. Rodney Richardson, Milo Ferguson, and Melvin Gartner. She shook her head at Melvin. *The barber was such an unassuming guy. What the hell was he doing there?* Two of the other bodies were identified as Hells Angels. She flashbacked to Richardson's face, the surprise, the shock, and the life leaving his eye. The body on its back in the field. A fresh clip upright in the stubble next to his assault rifle.

There was a knock at the door. She opened her eyes. The door opened. Robbie, her eight year old wore a red T-shirt, gelled brown hair, and a worried frown. Jackson, the youngest, rushed past his brother to her bedside, crawling up next to her.

"Careful Jackson. Your mom is hurting." Liam was the last in the room. He was just under six feet, still had most of his strawberry blond hair, had the same angelic facial features as the boys, and a pair of black rimmed glasses. "They wanted to be sure you're okay."

Robert stayed by the door.

Jackson pointed at her forehead. "What happened?"

She reached up to her hairline. "Some glass cut me."

Jackson asked, "How may stitches?"

She smiled as he nestled his head in against her neck.

"Seven I think."

The door opened, a uniformed officer poked his head in. "How you feelin' Knockers?" It was Larry Sutherland who was in his first year with the RCMP. He stepped inside. "Ouch!" He looked down at Robbie.

"Her name is Knox!" Robbie had his fists ready, his feet shoulder width apart, cheeks the colour of sunburn.

Larry had close-cropped black hair, stood close to six four, weighed at least two-thirty, and had a linebacker's body. "Sorry, Robbie. My mistake." He bent to rub a kneecap.

Sydney said, "I'm sorry. He shouldn't have kicked you. He just knows I hate being called that."

Larry pointed at his chest. "My bad." He held out his hand to Robbie. "Friends?"

Robbie crossed his arms.

"Robbie?" Sydney lifted her chin. "Go ahead."

Robbie offered a fist bump to Larry.

Liam asked, "Need us to leave?"

Larry nodded. "Just for a minute if you don't mind."

Liam picked Jackson up off the bed, kissed Sydney on the cheek, went over and held the door for Robbie. "Let's get some ice cream guys."

Larry waited for the door to shut. "I'm sorry Knox, I didn't know."

"Now you do."

Larry blushed.

Sydney smiled. "Look, you forget about charging Robbie for assaulting you, and I'll forget about what you said."

"Deal." Larry nodded, sitting in the chair next to the bed. "A superintendant from Calgary is here to interview you."

Sydney shrugged.

"I wanted to let you know there was a stockpile in the Quonset. Mostly meth, fentanyl, and coke. Looks like the meth was manufactured here, and the rest was transported in from BC along highways sixteen and eleven. There was a map in Milo's Expedition. Then Jean, the Corporation secretary, brought in a laptop from the town office, and said we should take a look. It belonged to Richardson. Some tech specialists are on their way from Edmonton to check it out."

"Anything else?" Sydney closed her eyes. *The shock and adrenaline are wearing off, I need some painkillers.*

"It looks like Richardson shot Thorpe and Gartner. The other victims died of shotgun wounds. A shotgun was next to Melvin's body."

She nodded. "Any idea why Melvin was there?"

"Word is he found out his son died. He got the news before the shooting."

"And he went after Richardson because of it?"

"And Milo. Word is Milo got Melvin's son hooked on meth."

If Milo did that to one of my boys, I'd probably do the same. "I think I'll take my boys home now." She put her feet on the floor, taking her time rising to stand. *No head spins. That's a good sign.*

"Did the doctor release you?" Larry took her elbow.

Sydney smiled. "Not yet but he will." She aimed herself for the door.

· · · · · · · · · · · · · · · ·

"How come you never told me about Marco and the Hells Angels?" Garrett sat in a lawn chair, drinking a glass of water in Fatima's back yard. The shade touched the wall of the stuccoed garage. The only green tree was a spruce. There were signs of buds on the Saskatoon bushes along the wall of the garage.

Fatima set down her glass of wine. "Do you want to know everything about what it was like to live with Marco? And do you want to tell me everything about what it was like with

Marie?”

Hell no. “Point taken.” He looked at the ice at the bottom of his glass, tipping the glass to his mouth.

“I want to know why you only drink coffee and water.” She raised her glass and took a sip. The red print of her lipstick remained.

“Booze gets my mouth going. I have no control over what I say. And I always wake up the next morning wondering why I decided to drink in the first place.”

She raised her eyebrows. “So you like to be in control?”

Garrett shrugged, chewing on an ice cube. “I just don’t like being a drunken asshole.”

Fatima took off her shoe, rubbing her toes up his shin.

I guess that was the right answer.

The back door opened. Dayna stepped onto the red brick patio. “What you two up to?”

There was a scuffing sound as Fatima put her foot back in her shoe.

Garrett thought, *Nothing now.* “What’s up?”

Dayna shook her head, pushing her fingers back through her shoulder length red hair, sitting down. “Just finished work on the beer cart and made two hundred in tips.”

Fatima said, “I think I’m in the wrong business.”

Garrett’s phone vibrated against his ribs. He lifted it out of his shirt pocket, setting it on speaker, putting it on the glass-topped table. “Hello?”

“Garrett?”

“Yes.”

Fatima went to sip her wine. Dayna took her mother’s glass and sipped.

“It’s Riley. I need a favour. Okay if Sam and I come and see you tomorrow?”

Garrett leaned forward as did the women. “What’s up?”

Riley’s voice was a Ritalin test rat on a wheel. “Sam’s been researching Kawasaki. It's nuts around here. Corporation is jammed with media vans and SUVs. Sam has this crazy idea he wants to run past you and says he needs your help."

Garrett asked. "What time?"

Riley hesitated. "What time's good for you? We gotta get out of here. Get some Calgary anonymity."

"How about lunch time? Want to go out and get a bite or you want me to make lunch?"

"Okay if we meet at your place?" Riley lowered his voice. "You're gonna think we're nuts."

"See you at noon."

Riley hung up.

Fatima asked, "Sam's going to buy a motorcycle?"

· · · · · · · · · · · · · · · ·

Three hours after Sydney Knox got home, there was a knock on the back door of their three-bedroom bungalow. She sat in the living room in the easy chair with her feet up and a London Fog on the nearby end table. Liam appeared from his office. "I'll take care of it." He walked though the kitchen.

Outside, on the front step, she could hear her son Robert. "My mom is resting. If you come any closer you will get wet."

Sydney got ready to sit up in case there was anything nasty said to her sons who insisted on protecting her from the journalists on the front sidewalk. So far, they'd sprayed one persistent reporter. Jackson, the youngest, did the honours. She recalled his laughter and smiled.

Liam opened the back door. "Hey Gwen, what's up?"

Sydney leaned forward, wincing at the muscle pain, easing to her feet. She shuffled over to the kitchen floor in her pink housecoat and bunny slippers.

Gwen said, "Just brought over some bison lasagna for you guys."

Sydney said, "Come on in Gwen. Want a cup of tea?"

She saw seven-year-old Michael poke his head around the doorframe. "Come on in Michael. The boys are having fun on the front step." He wore glasses, had his mother's green eyes, black hair, and university vocabulary. He ran up the stairs then to the front door. Gwen followed with a casserole dish she set on the stovetop.

Liam watched Sydney for a reaction.

Sydney smiled at him. "It's okay. Gwen and I'll talk for a few minutes, then I'll get some rest." She turned to Gwen. "Cup of tea?"

Gwen shook her head. Her pixie cut framed an angular jaw. She weighed about one thirty and was always immaculate. In fact she was, in many ways, the opposite of Sydney. Despite this, they had become friends within a month of Gwen's moving in next door.

Sydney led the way to the living room, easing her way into the easy chair. Gwen sat down on the couch, crossing one leg over the other. She wore black pants and a pale green blouse. Sydney asked, "What's up?"

Gwen shook her head. "Just getting away from the crowd. Can't get anything done down at the office. The phone is ringing, reporters coming in to pick my brain. People who wouldn't take my calls when I lost my job in Toronto are acting like old friends. So I came home to get some work done, think about what to do next, and cook some lasagna." She smiled, shaking her head. "And here I am whining when I should be asking how you are."

Tears came to Sydney's eyes. She reached up her sleeve for a tissue, wiping the moisture from her cheeks, then giving her nose a blow. Gwen got up, walking around the coffee table, hugging her friend.

Liam appeared with a box of tissues, setting it down next to Sydney, and rubbing her back with the flat of his palm.

Gwen looked up at him. "Sorry, I didn't come here to ..."

He held up his free hand. "She needed this. To let it all go."

After the sobbing stopped, Liam was back in his office, and Sydney could speak again, she said, "Sorry I got your blouse wet."

Gwen looked over at her shoulder. "I actually like the darker shade better."

"I shot him twice. Once in the mouth and once in the eye. He was wearing body armour. I've never killed anyone before. Then there were the other bodies. I walked to the scene after I made sure Richardson was dead and his assault rifle dismantled."

Gwen leaned forward on the couch with her elbows on her knees.

"Most were killed by Melvin's shotgun. The bodies were a mess. Melvin was stitched from the belly to the throat with automatic rifle wounds. He was such a gentle man."

Gwen asked, "You heard about his son? You knew Milo got him hooked on meth?"

Sydney took a deep breath, nodding.

Gwen looked over her shoulder. "Jean came to see me."

Sydney lifted her chin. Everybody in town knew Jean–the town's secretary–was the defacto mayor of Corporation. Rod was too busy drinking, snorting coke, schmoozing, and tooting his own horn to have time to perform the more mundane tasks associated with running Corporation. "She heard Melvin found out his son was dead. After that he went after Rod and Milo. It was a tipping point for Jean. She handed Rod's laptop over to the detachment."

"Not before she made copies of important emails and other documents." Gwen reached inside her pants pocket, pulling out a silver thumb drive. "And she wants to get together. Jean said, `What happened to Melvin should never have happened.' Apparently Jean's been gathering evidence.

It goes beyond Corporation. She was afraid of repercussions from Richardson and Milo before. Now, after Melvin and his son, she's pissed off and sick of being afraid."

SEVEN

<u>Tuesday, May 13</u>

G arrett looked at Ella. She was finger painting at the kitchen table. It was covered with newspapers, and she was protected by one of his old blue shirts. "We have guests for lunch, and they're meat eaters. What do you think of meatballs?"

Ella smiled, looked at her hands, wiping them across the chest of the paint shirt. "Done!" Then she lifted her arms away from the multi-coloured handprints.

It took fifteen minutes to get her cleaned up, changed, and her bag packed. They drove to the downtown Co-Op. Thankfully there was a red kid's cart with a pair of steering wheels and seatbelts. He sat Ella down, belting her in, and rolling toward the meat counter for ground bison and pork. "Cookie!"

He shook his head, rolling his eyes. "Ooops, sorry. Bakery first." He turned left, she steered right. They travelled to the bakery where a lady in a white outfit and hairnet smiled as she handed Ella a cookie. The toddler said, "Fanks."

They rolled over to the meat section. The woman behind the counter looked a year or two over twenty. She had red hair and a bemused smile. Garrett looked to his right. A grey haired lady in purple leaned to within two millimeters of his shoulder, staring at the ham. He looked to his left. A man wore a grey *Boogie Nights* hairpiece. He brushed up against Garrett's left arm. Garrett retreated through a gathering of a dozen seniors, all focused on the ham or the headcheese. Ella chewed on the cookie with one hand, steering with the other, and leaning her head from side to side to the beat of Michael Jackson's *Thriller* playing over the store's sound system. Garrett aimed her away from the Canada Pension Plan zombie meeting. Then Ella steered them to the roma tomatoes and onions while she sang, "Thrilla, thrilla nigh!"

After they got home, Ella was freshened up and in her booster chair. The groceries were unloaded, onions chopped and caramelizing in the pot. The door opened. Fatima walked in wearing her red dress and high heels. She kissed Ella on the cheek. "I had a cancellation and thought maybe you could use the help." She hugged Garrett from behind as he stirred the onions and poured in tomato sauce. "Smells great in here."

He grabbed the wooden spoon. "I just need to get this simmering, then I'll add the meatballs."

"How about if Ella and I have a chat?" Fatima turned, lifting Ella out of the booster chair.

Garrett washed his hands. He mixed hamburger and romano cheese with his hands, rolling individual meatballs to plop into the simmering sauce.

He finished up the last one and covered the pot as the sauce launched the occasional red lava lugi.

He went to the fridge, pulled out a bottle of Okanagan red wine, pouring Fatima a glass. She looked at it, looked at the time, shrugged and took a sip. "Thanks."

Garrett sat down on the couch next to Fatima. Only Ella's bum and legs were visible as she bent over the toy box, digging around, occasionally standing up to inspect a toy before dropping it on the carpet, and diving in to search some more.

They sat that way until the buzzer sounded. Fatima picked up the phone and pressed nine. Garrett got up, stopping the timer, going to the stove, and setting the water to boil for the penne. A knock on the door. Fatima opened it. Even though Sam and Riley were about the same height, they were a study in contrasts. Riley was grey haired and clean-shaven with a rather pointed nose flanked by grey eyes. Sam had a thick head of black hair, a full beard, and was round in the cheeks and belly. Garrett felt his ribs compress when they hugged him.

Riley asked, "How do you stand the city traffic?"

Sam said, "Smells great in here."

Ella got up, hustling over, and hiding behind Garrett's legs.

Riley crouched to see Ella eye to eye. She leaned right to see around Garrett's kneecap. Riley raised his eyebrows. Ella ducked from eyesight.

Fatima asked, "What would you like to drink?"

"Coffee?" Riley looked at Sam who nodded.

Garrett lifted Ella with his right arm. She hooked her hand in behind his bicep. "Lunch is almost ready."

Fatima sat across from Sam who settled onto the couch. She began, "I wanted to ask you about my daughter."

Riley stood next to Garrett as he ground the coffee beans and started the espresso machine. Ella kept looking at Riley then looking away. While he waited for the espresso machine to heat up, Garrett stirred the penne noodles.

Garrett asked, "What did you work on over the winter?"

"Another trebuchet. Someone in the States heard about mine and paid me to build it."

"Is it done?" Garrett steamed the milk then started the hot water filtering through the coffee grounds. He poured the milk over the espresso.

"Yep. The guy paid me to assemble it in California. Spent a month down there on a farm just north and east of San Diego."

Garrett pointed at the cups. Riley took one, walking over to Sam with the other. Sam looked up, smiled, took the cup, then nodded as Fatima said, "I'm just worried about my Dayna."

Pleasantries went back and forth until the timer went off. Garrett shut off the stove, draining the noodles. Fatima got up, placing the pot of meatballs on a hot plate in the middle of the oak table next to the kitchen. Garrett put Ella in her booster chair. He scooped some noodles into a teddy bear bowl, adding some sauce, and a meatball, before putting the bowl in the freezer. Three minutes later, Ella was busy using her fingers to fish for penne, everyone else had a full plate, and conversation stopped while they ate.

Fatima waved fingers in front of her mouth to help cool the hot centre of a meatball. She took a sip of wine. "What did you want to ask us about?"

Sam chewed as he covered his mouth. "I was hoping Garrett would help me with some videos and marketing."

Riley sat back, reaching for his coffee.

Fatima held her wine glass in both hands. Ella popped a noodle in her mouth. Garrett cut a meatball, soaking one half in the sauce on his plate. "What kind of marketing?"

"In July we're planning Corporation's First Annual Penis Festival, and we need to get the word out."

Fatima's eyebrows rose. She turned her head to look sideways at Sam.

Garrett stopped with the meatball one centimetre from his mouth.

Fatima pointed her fork at Sam. "I thought you wanted to buy a motorcycle."

It was Sam's turn to look puzzled.

Riley said, "He got the idea from the Penis Festival in Kawasaki, Japan."

"That explains the confusion." Fatima put her wine glass

down. "Will this be a family friendly event?"

Sam smiled refilling her glass. "Yes. The thing is we don't want Corporation to be remembered for a massacre. The whole town is in a state of shock. Laughter could be a way to help people to heal after the killings. We figure something outrageous like a penis festival would get people talking about things other than Richardson, his crowd, and the murders." He set the wine bottle down.

Garrett chewed his meatball. "What do you need me for?"

Riley picked up a piece of bread and buttered it. "People still watch your videos. Even three years after the fact they still watch you getting hit on the back of the head with a bottle of maple syrup. We figured if you helped us with some more videos it would help get people laughing and thinking about the town in a different way."

Fatima studied her wine glass. "Laughing with Garrett or at him?"

Sam considered the question. "Hopefully with him."

Ella hummed as she picked up another penne noodle and put it in the middle of her tomato sauce face.

Garrett looked at Ella and reached for a wet wipe. She lifted her left eyebrow and gave him a warning glare. He said, "Specifics, please."

Sam set his fork down. "Luke would do a video of you near Corporation's big sausage, we'd send it to media outlets, and put it on YouTube. You'd introduce the upcoming festival."

Garrett put the wet wipe down, looking at Fatima.

She asked, "Then what?"

Sam tented his fingertips. "It's not all planned yet, but we want to get the word out about the events."

"What are the events?" Fatima asked.

Ella began to hum *Thriller*.

Garrett had a flashback of seniors gathering around the

meat counter.

Riley said, "We're not sure yet."

Fatima leaned back. "When will it happen?"

Sam said, "July first."

Ella sang, "Thrilla, thrilla nigh!"

Garrett took a breath. "I'll do it." He turned, going in for a sneak attack with the wet wipe.

Ella swung her head from side to side. "Stop it! STOP IT!" Garrett managed two swipes. Ella gave him a Churchill-after-someone-stole-his-cigar glare.

"Isn't that the weekend we were planning to get married?" She pointed at Garrett. "Maybe you want to be married next to a forty foot sausage at a Penis Festival." Fatima put her hands on the table and stood. "Not me!"

Sam winked at her and smiled. "We could make it Corporation's First Annual Sausage Festival and Wedding?"

Fatima said, "Not happening."

· · · · · · · · · · · · · · ·

They arrived separately and on foot, otherwise someone in Corporation would notice the gathering at Jean's house. It would set tongues to wagging. Sydney took a short cut down the back alley. The mixture of sand and gravel was familiar under her feet. It felt good to be up and about and working bruised muscles. She found a steady pace allowed her to keep her breathing shallow so her ribs ached less. She thanked the Creator for the new ceramic bulletproof vest.

She turned right at the white garage, opening the chain link gate, walking up between the building and the garden. She stepped up onto the wooden deck attached to the back of the white house with the green trim around its windows and doors. She knocked on the screen. Jean said, "Come on in."

The hinges said nothing as Sydney opened the door, kicking off her open toed shoes. Jean smiled at her. She was fifty, grey haired, about five-foot three, and one hundred and twenty-five pounds of don't mess with me. Sydney wondered, not for the first time, what Rod Richardson had on Jean. She looked around the ten-foot by ten-foot kitchen. The cabinets were white, the counters were black, and the appliances stainless steel. That and the underlying aroma of lemon gave Jean's home a sparkling, efficient feel.

Jean wore black slacks and a blue blouse to accent her eyes. She poured coffee from a carafe into three cups, set them on a tray, and carried them through a doorway into the living room with the six by eight-foot window looking out onto Main Street. Well it would have looked out onto Main Street if the burgundy curtains were open.

They sat down at the round oak table. There were pictures on the wall of Jean's son, her daughter, and their families. It was a record of graduations, weddings, and births. "Rod threatened to hurt your kids didn't he?" Sydney reached for the cream.

Jean looked at the wall of pictures. "Not in so many words, but it was definitely implied. He used to say `The Angels have long arms.'"

Sydney stirred and sipped.

Jean looked at her. "When did you figure that out?"

"Just now."

Jean added sugar to her coffee. "They say you shot Rod's eyes out."

"Eye." She looked over the cup at Jean.

"How come you aimed for his eye?"

"The first one went in his mouth."

Jean frowned, waiting.

"He called me Knockers."

Jean nodded. "I almost wish I was there just to see it." There was a tap at the back door. "Come on in Gwen, it's open."

They heard the door swing. A pair of shoes slapped the linoleum. Gwen stepped into the living room. "Sorry I'm late." She set her red leather bag on the table, taking out a laptop. She opened it, powering up. She nodded in the direction of the third cup. "That mine?"

"Yep." Jean got up, returning with a full carafe. She glanced at Gwen's screen. "What did you find out?"

"Bits and pieces. The emails are interesting." She sipped her coffee then pointed at the screen. "Some of them are to a Nova Bank branch in Calgary."

Sydney leaned forward on her elbows.

Jean leaned over, pulling open a drawer in the maple china cabinet, retrieving a green folder. "Over the last year I made copies of emails and other correspondence." She opened the folder, sliding it in front of Sydney. Gwen leaned closer so she could see. "I think there's a pattern. On the fifteenth of each month Rod would get an email, then he would give me instructions on money transfers from one account to another. He also would get regular cheques from K&K Realty in Calgary."

Sydney asked, "Do you have copies of those transactions?"

Jean tapped the file. "They're here." She reached over to the cabinet, finding a collection of papers held together with a blue metal clip.

Gwen looked at Sydney. "Drug deals can be made through real estate purchases right?"

Sydney took the blue clipped pages. "That's right. The money and drugs never come together."

Jean lifted her chin.

Sydney pointed at the pages with her free hand. "A dealer, a distributer, or a manufacturer makes his money through real estate purchases resold for a two, three, or four hundred percent profit."

Jean asked, "Who owns K&K Realty?"

Gwen began to tap the keys on her laptop. "I'll see what I can find out."

Jean sat back, cradling her World's Best Momma coffee cup, looking at the pictures on the wall. "I had an interesting conversation with Riley."

Sydney asked, "As in Sam and Riley?"

Jean nodded. "They want to have a festival on Canada Day."

Gwen sat back as her laptop searched. "What kind of festival?"

"They want to call it Corporation's First Annual Penis Festival."

"What?" Sydney set her cup down.

Gwen smiled. "How are they going to get the word out?"

Jean looked puzzled. "They're in Calgary asking some guy named Garrett the Carrot or Parrot or something."

Gwen slapped her free palm on the table. "You're kidding!" She noted the blank faces. "You don't know do you?"

Sydney asked, "Know what?"

"He's a phenomenon. Just watch what happens when Garrett the Carrot's Penis Festival appears on social media." She tapped the side of her head with an index finger. "Riley and Sam are pretty savy."

Jean said, "I'm not too fussy about the name."

Gwen asked, "Why not? It might help us bring down the drug dealing, bullshitting, swinging dicks who turned this town into hub of illegal activity."

Sydney tapped her forefinger on the rim of her coffee cup. "Maybe Sausage Festival would be better. A little more subtle." She stuck her tongue in the side of her cheek.

Jean covered her smile.

EIGHT

Wednesday, May 14

0

Y ou wanna what?" Jacolynne said as she slid Ella into her booster chair. Fresh strawberries and blueberries were arranged on a plate. Ella's hair stuck out at just-woke-up angles. She frowned at the plate then took a strawberry between her thumb and forefinger. Ella looked at Garrett, raising her eyebrows. He nodded. She took a bite.

"I want to take Ella to Corporation this Friday if it's okay with you." Garrett leaned his backside against the counter, keeping one eye on his granddaughter.

Jacolynne wore a black T-shirt and pants. There were peach flats on her feet. Her black hair was brushed back, and her face free of makeup. She shook her head, looking at Ella. "You sure it's safe up there?"

"Jac, I'm going to visit Riley and Sam. They asked me for some help."

Jac took one of Ella's strawberries. "With what?"

Oh hell, go for it. "Sam is planning a sausage festival."

Jac stopped chewing, placing her hand over her mouth. "A what?"

"He and Riley have this plan to have a sausage festival so people will think Corporation is a place where people celebrate instead of a place where a massacre occurred."

"What kind of sausage are we talking about?"

"Sam saw a YouTube video of a festival in Japan. It got him thinking."

Jac swallowed. "Why do they need you?"

He shrugged, pointing at his chest. "Garrett the Carrot."

"You mean more videos?"

"Some promotion to get the word out about the festival."

Jac turned her head to the right, looking at him with that annoying `Come on, spill it' look of hers.

"They want me to pose in front of Corporation's sausage and talk while they make a video."

She nodded. "Just keep Ella out of the video." She looked at the stove clock. "I gotta go. Okay if I pick her up at four thirty?" Jac was out the door before he could answer.

He looked at smiling Ella with blueberry purple on her chin and cheeks. "How about a road trip?"

NINE

<u>Thursday, May 15</u>

O

Sydney met Loraine Starlight on Main Street in Cochrane. Loraine was waiting at Abe's Shawarma Shop. Loraine was a slender, dark-haired, dark-eyed Medical Examiner from Calgary with a taste for exotic flavours and wild meat. As Sydney opened the door, Loraine said, "When you gonna put some buffalo on the menu Abe?"

Abe was thirty something, wore a white T-shirt, had short black hair, and a pronounced jaw line. He stood behind the glass display case with columns of beef and chicken roasting and rotating behind him. "As soon as you catch one for me, it'll be on my rotisserie."

Sydney sat across from Loraine at a red table next to the window. "Thanks for meeting me."

Loraine smiled. "It's supper time, and I haven't had a donair in months." She looked around, leaning across the table until she was close to touching noses with her friend. "You okay?" She looked at the stitches on Sydney's forehead. "I heard you got shot."

Sydney tapped her sternum. "I was wearing my new vest. I was lucky. Why don't we order?"

"Already done. Don't change the subject." Loraine leaned

back. "I thought you wanted to know about the autopsies."

"I do."

"But you don't want to talk about what happened to you?"

Sydney said, "Not much to tell. The truck's windshield was hit, I was hit, then I drove off the road, and into a field. I got out and hid behind the engine while the mayor of Corporation stitched up my unit. He got close. I heard him reloading, stood up, and shot him."

"Once in the mouth. Once in the eye." Loraine was studying her. Those eyes had appraised Sydney the first time they'd met in a Calgary high school. A couple of grade ten First Nation's girls in a strange land of football players, cliques, outcasts, drama kids, drama queens, wannabees, don't wannabees, and overriding frustrated horniness.

"How come you shot him that way?"

"He called me `Knockers'." Sydney spotted Abe coming around from behind the counter with two plates and two donairs. She lifted her chin. "Thank you."

Abe set the plates in front of the women. "Want something to drink?"

Loraine looked up, smiling. "We'll grab them in a minute."

"Enjoy." Abe walked back to the end of the counter.

Loraine peeled back the white and black checkered paper tightly wrapped around the donair and took her first bite.

Sydney got to work on her falafel with its crunchy fritters and pickled vegetables. She closed her eyes. "Missed these."

Loraine reached for a napkin, wiping her lips. "Five of the deceased died from shotgun wounds. The police officer and the barber died of multiple gunshot wounds. Richardson, well you know how he died."

"So, Gartner did shoot five."

"Why was the barber even there?"

Sydney wiped her lips with a napkin. "He found out his son died. The son was an addict. The word is that Milo

Ferguson, Richardson's partner, got the boy hooked. Melvin was this kind, friendly, reliable, caring, and hard working guy who never missed a day's work at the shop. He left the barbershop that morning, drove out to Richardson's acreage, and shot five people. Apparently two of them were Angels, and the other three worked for Richardson." Sydney shook her head, setting the falafel on her plate. "I don't know what I would do if I lost one of my boys."

"It's starting to hit you now. A delayed reaction?"

Sydney wiped her eyes. "I think so." She lifted the falafel, began working at tearing back the paper wrapped around the bread, taking a bite. Her phone rang. She lifted it out of her pants pocket, looking at Loraine.

She said, "Go ahead. This is good." She took another bite of her donair.

"Hello?" Sydney set the falafel down, putting the phone to her ear.

"It's Gwen. There's been a development."

"What kind?" Sydney looked at Loraine.

"I was at the Shell station. Doug Brown just arrived in town."

"Who's he?"

"The Krotch brother's charming psychopathic fixer."

"This isn't funny."

Gwen said, "I'm not joking."

TEN

Friday, May 16

O

Garrett's Ford rumbled over the train tracks on the south side of town. He looked at the dash clock. Fifteen minutes before he was due to meet Sam and Riley at Corporation's sausage statue. The wind blew across the highway, bending the budding trees east. The sky was blue grey. Clouds hung out about five hundred metres above the ground. The car rocked in a wind gust. Ella snored in her car seat. Garrett inhaled, sniffing the initial hint she was in need of freshening up.

He turned into the Shell station, got out, and filled up his car. Garrett watched his granddaughter through the glass. Her head was tipped back and her mouth open. *She's perfect.*

He kept his eyes on her even while walking into the front door of the station where chips, pop, and chocolate bars lined a two metre wide pathway to the cash register. The woman behind the counter had her long brown hair tied back in a ponytail, accessorized with green eyes, green blouse, and a smile. "Mornin'."

Garrett reached into his pocket, pulling out a fifty. "Good morning. Does your washroom have a change table?"

She took the bill. "No but Woody's does." She leaned

her head in the direction of the café on the other side of the pumps. "Food's good."

"And the coffee?" He took the change.

"The best." The woman looked at his car. "How old?"

"Almost two years."

"You're Garrett aren't you?" She pointed at him. "Sam said you might stop by. Thanks for helping us out. Things have been crazy. Most of the TV trucks and reporters have moved on, thank God. We went from being a quiet little place to scandal central." She handed him his change.

He backed toward the door. "Thanks. I'd better get her cleaned up." He saw the cashier reach for the phone as he went outside. Ten minutes later, Ella sat next to him in a high chair. She looked around at the solid oak tables, solid oak chairs, oak trimmed walls, windows, and oak counter separating the kitchen from the customers. The toddler raised her eyebrows, looking at Garrett whose hands were damp from three washings. He sniffed the back of his right hand as the waitress arrived. She was forty with dyed black hair, a full figure accented by a white blouse, and pink camel toe sweats. She carried a carafe of coffee, lifting it at Garrett, and raising her eyebrows. He nodded. She walked over, filling his cup. "Want a menu?" She smiled at Ella.

He nodded. "Thank you. Could we get a plate of fries, and do you have any fresh fruit, please?"

"Strawberries and bananas?" She bent to eye level with Ella. "Do you like pancakes?"

Ella smiled.

"Okay. Pancakes, strawberries, bananas, and fries, please," Garrett said.

The waitress looked at him. "You're Garrett."

"Yes." *I forgot how word gets around in Corporation.*

"Thanks for coming." She walked back to the kitchen while he doctored his coffee, reaching into Ella's diaper bag, and handing her a bottle of milk.

A man weighing maybe one hundred and sixty pounds and standing five ten pulled out a chair, sitting across from Garrett. "Mind if I join you?" His hair was blonde, moustache immaculately military-trimmed, voice radio smooth. "I'm new in town. Maybe you can help me out. I'm Doug Brown."

Garrett looked behind Doug's rectangular glasses. *I know your type. That's what happens from thirty years of working with people, you can spot a psychopath a kilometre away.* He turned to Ella whose eyes watched Doug from behind the bottle. She glanced at her grandfather. *Play along Ella.* He looked at Doug's worn brown leather jacket, and the blue golf shirt he wore underneath. His jeans were a bit too clean, and his cowboy boots made of exotic leather. *I've met people like you before. Taught a few. Sat across the table at parent teacher interviews with some. Worked under a principal with that same arrogant, self-assured absence of empathy. The charm is a clear nail polish façade.* "What can I do for you?"

Doug smiled.

Garrett looked right, seeing Ella stick her tongue out, putting her lips together. Someone chuckled. He turned some more and faced a blue eyed, grey haired woman of approximately fifty who was the shortest adult in the café. He sensed all eyes looking up to her. She stuck out her hand. "I'm Jean."

Garrett stood, shaking her hand. "I'm Garrett. This is Ella."

Jean asked, "May I?" She sat facing Ella with her back to Doug. "How are you this morning?"

Ella nodded, air escaping from the bottle's nipple. "Good."

Jean looked confused for a moment. "How old is she?"

"Nearly two."

Jean raised her eyebrows.

Garrett shrugged. *What can I say? It's obvious she's bright. And if I tell you she's eighteen months, you'll think she's a freak.*

Ella pointed at Doug. "Phithead."

Garrett blushed.

Doug said, "My name's ..."

Jean interrupted, "I know who you are Mr. Brown. You work for the Krotch brothers. The little one is right. You are a shithead." She smiled at Ella.

Doug smiled. "I think you have me confused with someone else."

Jean turned to face him. "There is no confusion. You do the Krotch brother's dirty work. You're here to determine what can be salvaged from Rod's operation."

Doug gave her a blank look. "You have a very active imagination."

Jean rolled her eyes, turning her back on him. The waitress arrived with fries and fruit. Ella smiled. Garrett moved his chair closer to Ella.

Doug stood up. "I'll leave you to your meal."

He makes it sound like he's doing us a favour. Garrett peeled Ella's banana while she took a bite out of a strawberry.

Jean said, "Thank you for agreeing to help us."

"Riley and Sam are family." He took a closer look at her, seeing the intelligence behind those blue eyes, and something else, sadness perhaps.

"At first I thought Sam's idea was crazy, but then I realized he's exactly right. We need a different kind of reputation and a party. This town's in mourning right now–mostly about what happened to Melvin–but that will change. In a month or so, summer will brighten our mood, and we'll be ready."

Garrett picked up a french fry, blew on it, handing it to Ella. "The lady at the Shell station called you?"

Jean nodded. "That's Shelly. I asked her to keep an eye out."

He picked up another fry, testing it for heat. "Riley says you've been the real mayor here for longer than Richardson."

She looked around the café where some people pretended

not to listen while others stared. One man in a ball cap even cupped his hand over an adjacent ear. Jean smiled at Garrett, raising her eyebrows.

Garrett tried another approach. "How did you know Doug Brown works for the Krotch brothers?"

She picked up a fry, blew on it, handing it to Ella. "I have my sources."

So the café is where you get the news out to the town. No press releases, just talk about it here. In half an hour the whole town will know Doug works for the Krotch boys. He looked at the clock above the counter. "I'm late to meet with Sam and Riley."

She put her free hand up, lifting her chin, and smiling. "Don't worry. They know where you are."

The waitress brought a cup for Jean and refilled Garrett's coffee. Jean said, "Thanks Sue."

Sue handed him more creamers. "More fries?"

He looked at the empty plate then at Ella who nodded. He said, "Yes, please."

Jean sipped, and sat back. "You ever hear of Giles Patriot?"

"The alchoholic with the radio show?" Garrett stirred his coffee.

"His show goes from eleven to three. My guess is that's where Mr. Brown is headed. In half an hour or so you'll be asked to join Giles in his studio."

"And?"

"You will have a decision to make." She looked at Ella. "You will have plenty of volunteers to babysit this one if you decide to say yes."

He shook his head, exhaling slowly. *Holy shit! Not even noon, and I'm in it up to the neck.*

Ella began to laugh.

An hour later she was howling after twenty minutes of being outside in the biting wind. They stood out front of

Corporation's forty-foot erection honouring the sausage. The winter had chipped off some of the paint at the tip. A pair of manicured spruce trees trimmed into spheres straddled the sculpture. Luke–the town's filmmaker–had finished with the video clip. They headed for the cars where Ella stopped howling, promptly closing her eyes and snoring.

Garrett followed Riley to the north side of town where a telecommunications tower was nicknamed the town's Bigger Erection or the Big E. Beneath it sat a white concrete block of a building with a red roof and a billboard. The ad on the sign was bigger than the building. A two-storey image of Patriot's fleshy face, dyed black hair, and the words, All Truth All the Time.

Riley parked next to a lone blue Buick. Luke climbed out the Ford's passenger door while Garrett parked a couple of metres away. He got out, took his time releasing Ella, lifting her out of the car with her nestling against his neck. Riley held open the door. Luke stood on the other side. He looked like his head might bump the top of the door if he didn't duck. Luke had short black hair, a quilt-lined jean jacket, a red and black prairie dinner jacket, jeans, and tan work boots. He pointed at the blue fleece vest he'd brought for Garrett to wear. "It's all set. All you need do is keep facing him."

Garrett nodded, handed Ella to Riley, slipped on the vest, then walked inside. The second set of glass doors were locked. They had to wait for an athletic man with blonde hair parted down the middle, broad shoulders, a tight blue T-shirt, and black jeans. He opened the door. "You MacGregor?"

Garrett nodded.

Riley said, "This is Billy Pendergrast."

Billy looked at Riley then at Ella and Luke. "You guys can wait on the couch with the kid."

Riley followed them through the doors. Garrett set Ella's change bag next to the black leather couch. He followed

Pendergrast into the far corner of the building where two extra interior walls made a square soundproof room with one door and one window. Billy's smaller square room pressed up against the left side of the door. Pendergrast put his index finger to his lips then opened the door for Garrett. He walked into the soundproofed room lined with thousands of tiny grey triangles of foam. The door closed behind him. Giles Patriot sat at the far side of a table with four microphones attached to metal elbows. The room smelled of mint mouthwash with underlying hints of second-hand alcohol. He wore a pair of black headphones. His black hair was gelled. The hairs at the top of his head were planted in rows. His cheeks were river systems of red veins. A double chin hung below a half moon of what was once a jaw line. There were shiny wet semi circles under the arms of his black shirt. His grey eyes attempted to focus on Garrett. Patriot nodded in the general direction of the only other chair in the room. Garrett saw it had four wheels.

Giles pointed to the microphone in front of Garrett. "Talk and I'll check your levels."

Garrett leaned closer to the mic. "About what?"

"Sounds good. We're on the air."

Garrett looked at Giles who smiled, pointing a bratwurst finger. "This morning we have Garrett MacGregor, better known as Garrett the Carrot. You'll remember his fifteen seconds of fame from about three years ago. In the first video the famed journalist and Order of Canada recipient, Elizabeth Chevrolet hit him over the head with a bottle. Then he rescued his brother from a burning truck. We all hoped his lackluster attempts at fame were over, but it appears he's planning a comeback. Tell my audience why you're here."

Garrett hesitated. "I'm here to help Corporation promote an upcoming festival."

"Oh yes, a cockamamie plan dreamed up by Riley our resident eccentric and his partner Sam."

Garrett heard the sarcasm when Giles used the word `partner'. He felt his face flush.

"The delightful pair have decided we should all get together and celebrate the sausage! And whose sausages will be at this festival? Yours Mr. MacGregor?" Giles voice was rising now, overfull with sarcasm. "I'm sure it will be a very short celebration."

Garrett found some words. "I'll be there, enjoying Corporation's famous sausage and other events the town is able to attract."

"I'll make a prediction right now. No one will come to your obscene little festival, because no one will be able to stomach the way you and your buddies have exploited our tragedy!"

"No one's being exploited. In fact it's just the opposite."

Giles began to spit on the papers in front of him. "I'm sick of pinko liberals like you coming into this town and exploiting us!" He farted but seemed not to notice. "Get the hell off my show, and get the fuck out of town before I get a gun and shoot you myself!"

Garrett stood up. His chair tipped over.

"He's attacking me!" Giles picked up a binder, throwing it at Garrett. The binder broke apart. A barrage of paper zigged and zagged over the consul.

Garrett backed up to the door, opening it.

"I'm being attacked by a fuckin' terrorist!"

Garrett shut the door.

"Got it." Luke closed his laptop, following behind Riley and Ella. They went out the first set of doors then the second. It took only a minute to get Ella secured in her seat. They left the parking lot with Patriot's two-storey toothy grin looking down on them. Garrett drove south of town then east to Sam and Riley's place. The house was a hundred-year-old cream coloured, two-storey Eaton's catalogue special their grandfather had built.

Ella was awake by the time the video was downloaded from the camera nestled in the chest pocket of the fleece vest. Garrett looked around the kitchen, inhaling the scent of milk from the separator just outside the door, and the aroma of wood burning in the black and white cast iron kitchen stove. He rubbed his hand over the arm of his grandfather's favourite oak chair.

Ella knelt in the chair, eating and keeping an eye on the location of her grandfather.

Riley busied himself around his latest creation; a galvanized pail for a reservoir, an electric heating element suspended inside, coiled quarter inch copper pipe, a portafilter with wrench handle, a steam nozzle from an air seeder, and a grinder adapted from a differential. He finished the first latte, setting it in front of Garrett who sipped expecting an after taste of petroleum products. There was none. He smiled. "This is awesome."

Sam smacked his palms together. "Riley said you would be the true test of his new espresso machine. He's happy now!"

Riley looked over his shoulder, smiling.

Luke asked, "When do you want to put the Patriot video up?"

Sam looked at Riley who finished up another latte, handing the steamer to Sam. Riley asked, "Right away?" He looked at his cousin.

Garrett looked at Ella who was shaking her head from side to side. "No, I think we should wait. Let's see if Patriot digs himself a hole we can bury him in."

Luke asked, "Whadya mean?"

Garrett pointed at Sam. "You said Patriot was in tight with Richardson right? That he was like the mayor's enabler and promoter. Patriot'll make a big deal about what just happened. So we let him dig himself in deep with his version of the story, then we release the video." He took a sip of coffee. "Can I have another one of these?" He glanced at Ella. "Please."

Luke's eyebrows met in the middle.

ELEVEN

<u>Saturday, May 17</u>

0

YYC News
<u>Social Media Star Returns</u>

Garrett the Carrot (Garrett MacGregor) has made a return to social media and is already creating fresh controversy. There is a new video of Garrett promoting the upcoming Sausage Festival in Corporation, Alberta. He stands in front of Corporation's phallic sculpture, promoting the town's upcoming Canada Day celebrations.

Almost simultaneously, Corporation's shock jock Giles Patriot accused Garrett of exploiting Corporation's tragedy and assaulting him at the town's radio station.

Two years ago Garrett MacGregor became a social media phenomenon after being hit over the head by Elizabeth Chevrolet. After initially denying the assault, the one time Calgary columnist resigned when a video of the attack surfaced. Subsequent videos of Garrett also went viral.

We asked Garrett for a response to Patriot's allegations and he said, "Yes I met with Giles. No I did not assault him."

Giles Patriot said, "I am going to make sure that terrorist Garrett the Carrot goes to jail."

. . . .

After a week of early morning wake ups and chasing a toddler around, Saturday morning sleep-ins became Garrett's guilty necessity. The phone rang at seven thirty. He reached over, knocking the phone onto the floor, flipping back the covers. He got to his feet, bending over, picking up the phone.

Fatima said, "Your balls are hanging around your knees. Put on some pants and close the blinds!"

Garrett said, "Hello."

Jacolynne said, "That didn't take long."

Garrett crouched down, crabbing sideways, reaching for the cord to close the bedroom blinds. "What are you talking about?"

"You're in the news again. Something about you, Corporation, and some guy named Patriot. He actually called you a terrorist?"

He sat down at the end of the bed. "That and some other things. He was pretty drunk."

"Where was Ella at the time?"

"With Riley outside the studio. She slept through it all.""

"She woke up at six thirty, and she has a new word."

"What's that?"

"Fries. She wants fries for breakfast."

"Oh, sorry."

"It's okay dad. Is it normal for a kid to have that kind of vocabulary at eighteen months? She's using complete sentences."

"I was wondering that too. I thought it usually happened after three or four years."

"I'm worried about it dad."

"Worried about her talking?"

"Worried about her being too smart."

Garrett caught himself before laughing. "I wouldn't worry

about Ella, she seems to have it all under control."

"What?"

"I just trust her advice and things work out."

"Are you nuts?"

He thought about it for a moment. "Well, yes. But the kid lets you know what she wants. And when I'm about to make a decision I watch for her reaction. If I do what she tells me, things tend to work out. It makes her happy, and we get along."

"Oh I thought you meant you actually ask for her opinion or something like that."

I do, but it sounds like you're not ready to hear that.

"David's coming over to babysit Ella while we go to a movie."

"How's he doing?" Garrett looked in the mirror, seeing Fatima getting up and moving to sit next to him. She held his shorts out, perching them overtop of his junk.

"Sad. But I'll know more tonight."

Garrett felt the warmth of Fatima next to him. "You figured Melissa out. She had me fooled."

"She had a lot of people fooled dad. I got a bad feeling from her. David always had to make compromises and be on call when she needed something. She was stringing him along."

"Let me know how he is. Maybe you all could come over for supper tomorrow, or something?"

Jacolynne said, "I'll talk with David and Mark then get back to you. Bye dad. And dad?"

"Yeah?"

"Don't end up in the hospital like you did last time."

"I'll try." They hung up.

Fatima put her hand on his shoulder. "David okay?"

Garrett shrugged. "I hope so." He turned to her. "I should have asked you first about inviting them over."

She smiled. "I'll forgive you if you invite Dayna and Siobhan. Go make the coffee. I've got to open up in an hour."

TWELVE

<u>Sunday, May 18</u>

0

Garrett took a burger off the grill, put it on a plate. He took a bite. He smiled, popping the other half in his mouth. He looked out at the traffic on Kensington Road. It was a Sunday afternoon mix of cars, motorcyclists set to cruise the Kensington district, and cyclists working on their legs to get in shape for the summer. He bent down, shutting off the propane. He set the burgers onto a platter and thunked the barbecue lid shut. He stepped inside. The kids sat on the couch or at the table with Ella who was in her high chair enjoying blue berries and the attentions of Dayna and Siobhan. Fatima set a Mediterranean salad on the counter, reached into the fridge for a bottle of wine. She held up the opener. "Food's ready. Who wants wine?"

"Me please." David stood up from the easy chair where he'd been watching a preview of the NFL season. Mark talked about the movie he was working on. He went to a cupboard and grabbed two wine goblets. "Just the two?"

Siobhan put up an index finger, smiling. David retrieved a third glass as Jacolynne, Fatima, David, Mark, and Garrett all moved to find their spots at the table.

Garrett poured himself a glass of water doctored with

quartered limes and ice cubes. Dayna lifted her glass, and he poured water for her while Fatima poured wine for Mark and Siobhan. Food was passed, buns were buttered, condiments added, mastication began. Ella concentrated on her blue berries. Peace was a lazy dog in the corner. Jacolynne said, "Marie and Fergus are talking about moving to Calgary. They say they want a fresh start after their divorces."

Garrett looked at his salad. Ingredients fresh from the farmer's market, all delightful in their own way. He set his fork down. Appetite was drying dog shit on an August sidewalk. He caught Fatima's sideways glance.

Mark said, "That was a definite conversation killer."

Jacolynne's tone cut across three lanes of emotion, merging into defensiveness. "How would you have said it then?"

Mark looked at Ella whose head lifted when she heard the shift in tone. "Marie called this morning. Jac's been worried all morning about how to break the news."

Siobhan looked at Dayna. Jac saw the question in Siobhan's eyes, so she pointed a finger at her heart. "Marie is my mother and David's. Fergus is my Dad's brother, and my dickhead biological father. My mom just got a divorce from my Dad's other brother Murdock, after she got caught screwing around with Fergus – again." She lifted her eyebrows, focusing on Siobhan. "Do you detect a pattern here?"

Siobhan blinked, using her right hand to push a wayward strand of black hair behind her ear. "That's …"

"Messed up?" David shook his head. "Welcome to the family?"

Fatima went for her wine glass. "Marco threatened to get the Hells Angels after Garrett if he didn't break it off with me. But it looks like Marco's Hells Angels connection was wiped out in Corporation."

Dayna said, "Shit Mom, why didn't you tell me?"

Fatima sipped her wine, wiping her lips with a napkin, and lifting the glass to the light to inspect the red grape's legs. "I was saving it for the right moment." She clicked her tongue at her daughter. Dayna shook her head. "And this is definitely the right moment."

David leaned across, looking at Siobhan. "Got any dirty family undies to share?"

Fatima took a sip of wine.

Ella said, "Bergus is a dick!"

Fatima choked. She reached for a napkin to catch the wine from her nose.

Jac blushed. "Ella!"

Siobhan patted Fatima on the back, handing her another napkin.

David raised his glass. "Cheers to Ella who always knows exactly the right thing to say. Fergus definitely is a dick." He turned to his father. "So Dad, speaking of dicks, what exactly is the plan for the *Sausage* Festival?"

Garrett shrugged. *Good question.*

THIRTEEN

<u>Monday, May 26</u>

O

There's something to be said for the first day the temperature gets up over twenty and the sun warms your face. Sydney walked the back alley to Jean's house. She looked for any curious faces peering from behind bedroom curtains or through kitchen windows. *It'll be more private when all the trees and hedges get some leaves on them.* She turned to open Jean's gate, spotting some tulips poking out of the black earth along the sidewalk. She knocked on the back door.

"It's open!" Jean said.

As Sydney kicked off her shoes, Gwen said, "Coffee's in here and we've got Nanaimo bars." Sydney walked through the kitchen then into the living room. Gwen wore a blue blouse. Jean had a floral patterned sundress. Sydney felt out of place in her black T-shirt and khaki shorts.

Gwen poured her a coffee from the carafe. "Jean's found something interesting."

Sydney pulled out a chair, sat, added cream and sugar to her coffee, and stirred.

Jean pushed a red file folder over to Sydney. "I ran hard copies at the town office. They are emails between Rod and the Krotch brothers."

Sydney opened the file and began to read.

• • • • • • • • • • • • • • • •

"Is the hole deep enough? Luke wants to know." Riley was on his cell phone, and it sounded like he was driving his vintage Ford on a gravel road with the windows open. Either that or he was shaking a can of marbles.

"What was that?" Garrett stuck his left finger in his ear. Ella sat on the living room floor, humming a tune, and hammering a round wooden dowel into a square hole.

"I said, is Patriot's hole deep enough? Luke asked me to ask you! Patriot spent the entire week making threats, promising a lawsuit for the damage done to his studio, calling us terrorists, and country con artists. We want to know when we can release the video of what really happened."

Garrett smiled as Ella gave the dowel an almighty whack. "Why not today?"

"Good. And Sam has some news. He'll call you tomorrow."

FOURTEEN

<u>Tuesday, May 27</u>

O

YYC News

A video of the actual interview between Giles Patriot and Garrett MacGregor contradicts Patriot's portrayal of the event. The video shows Patriot throwing various objects, berating MacGregor, and accusing him of assault.

Since the interview aired on Patriot's Corporation Radio program, he has maintained MacGregor assaulted and threatened him. No evidence of Patriot's accusations appears on the video.

Mr. Patriot refused to comment on the video. When a camera crew and reporter tried to interview him at the Corporation Hotel Bar, he left out a back door. After Patriot tripped and fell, he said, "I'm the victim here. MacGregor attacked me in my studio." Patriot proceeded to vomit on the reporter's shoes.

The local RCMP detachment's Constable Raye Lennox said, "The alleged assault is part of an ongoing investigation, and we are looking at the video as part of that investigation."

. . . .

"Hey Garrett it's Sam. I just had a very interesting

conversation with Ruby Dodginghorse. She's an elder at the Coyote Lake Reservation. An old friend of my mom's."

Garrett sat on the couch with the phone tucked up in between his ear and left shoulder. Ella was nestled in the crook of his right elbow. She sucked on her bottle then stopped. The air wheezed out of the bottle's nipple.

"Okay," Garrett whispered.

"I've been phoning around telling people about the festival and asking for their support."

Garrett watched Ella's eyelids for any fluttering.

Sam said, "Anyway, I got a hold of Eva. She's a big fan of yours. When I told her about the video showing Patriot throwing stuff around his studio, she got real interested. Patriot's one of those guys who likes to use the First Nations as scapegoats. Says they waste taxpayer's money. He also has plenty of horribly stereotypically racist things to say under the guise of free speech. Anyway, Eva took a look at today's video, and she thinks there might be some interest in holding a rodeo at the festival."

"Cool."

"You there?"

Garrett turned his head to the right, the phone fell, and he had to fish it out from between two cushions. "Sorry, Sam. Ella's asleep. Just trying not to wake her."

"No problem. Just thought I'd let you know about this development."

"Thanks."

"And there might be another group interested."

Garrett heard the hesitation in Sam's voice. "Who's that?"

"One of the welders in town is a drag queen. I mean not many people know it, but she called and asked if she could run an idea past her friends in Calgary."

"And?"

"She'll get back to me in a day or two."

93

FIFTEEN

Wednesday, May 28

0

He sat next to Ella under the skylight in the mall's food court with the surrounding hum of conversation. The scent of something Szechuan made Garrett turn to the distinctive sound of metal on wok.

Ella had her eye on another toddler, rolling by in a stroller. The mom talked on her cell phone.

Garrett spotted Sam and a woman headed his way. The woman wore jeans, a long-sleeved floral-patterned shirt, and running shoes. She was as tall as Sam who wore a blue and black checkered prairie dinner jacket and worn-to-pale-blue jeans. Garrett waved. Sam smiled and approached.

The woman's expression remained unchanged. She appeared to be a little bit older than Garrett's fifty-seven but wind and winters had left a relief map on her face. He noticed her grey hair was tied back in a ponytail reaching the belt at the back of her jeans.

Garrett stood and waited. Sam walked closer, stopped, and said, "This is Ruby Dodginghorse."

Do I shake her hand? Instead Garrett found himself engulfed in a hug. He caught the comforting scent of sage as Ruby released him and bent to face Ella who smiled then said, "Hi."

Conversation didn't begin until Ella had a strawberry smoothie, Ruby had a London fog, and Garrett and Sam had coffees. Ruby asked, "Who will be able to enter the rodeo?"

Garrett looked at Sam who asked, "Who wants to enter?"

"Some boys, some girls, some men, some women." Ruby studied them through the steam from her London fog.

"You mean you want a rodeo where men and women compete equally?" Sam smiled.

Ruby nodded.

Garrett thought, *Why not?*

Sam asked, "Which events were they wanting?"

Ruby set her cup down, helping Ella who had pulled the straw out of her drink, and was having difficulty reinserting. "Cutting, barrel racing, calf roping."

Garrett shrugged.

Sam said, "Works for me."

Ruby turned to Garrett, waiting. He wiped Ella's chin. "What do you need me to do?"

Ruby shrugged.

Sam said, "Eva's not going to tell you what to do."

Garrett looked at Ella. Her blue eyes were focused on him. "It should be the opposite of exclusive. Richardson had his clique of friends, and they ran the town. The Krotch brothers want their views heard and others drowned out. Patriot attacks any ideas different from his own. It would be great if the festival's answer was open events."

Sam watched Ruby who was tickling Ella's cheek with the bent forefinger of her right hand. Ella smiled, closing her eyes. Ruby said, "This little one is very bright." She turned to Garrett. "I think open events would work well."

Ella smiled, pointing first at Garrett then Ruby. "Good idea."

. . . .

YYC News

<u>Drugs, Weapons Found at Corporation Crime Scene</u>

The RCMP held a news conference in Corporation, Alberta this morning. Constable Raye Lennox released new information about the recent mass killing.

Lennox said, "One hundred and thirty kilos of cocaine and over twenty thousand methamphetamine and fentanyl tablets were found on site at the Richardson property. A cache of handguns, assault rifles, ammunition, and body armour was also found in a Quonset hut on the property."

When asked for more information about the shooting victims, Lennox said, "That investigation is ongoing, and the information will be released at a later date."

Corporation, Alberta was the site of a mass shooting on May 12 of this year. Eight bodies were found at the scene including Mayor Rodney Richardson and fourteen-year RCMP veteran Constable Bill Thorpe. Another RCMP officer was wounded on the scene. She is reported to be recovering at home.

SIXTEEN

<u>Friday, May 30</u>

O

Upper Canada Press
<u>Corporation: The Story Behind the Story</u>

By Elizabeth Chevrolet

The recent tragedy in Corporation, Alberta is a simple story. One local drug lord is taking over territory from another.

A shrewd plan is being revealed under the guise of a Canada Day Festival. A local resident and known drug supplier is making his move to fill the vacuum left by the death of Milo Ferguson. Sam Sieben, a longtime resident of the area, is a known grower and supplier of marijuana to locals. It is becoming apparent that Sam, like most successful entrepreneurs, recognizes an opportunity to expand his operation.

His brainchild is Corporation's cynical Sausage Festival. Sam plans to use Canada's birthday to sell his product to celebrants. This is undoubtably the most blatantly immoral exploitation of our nation's birthday since Confederation.

SEVENTEEN

<u>Sunday, June 1</u>

0

"So they're going after Sam now." Gwen poured coffees for her friends as they sat around her kitchen table. The sun shone through a pair of windows.

Jean wore a blue sweater. She looked out the window at the grey clouds.

Sydney wore a grey hoodie. "The rain is turning everything green."

Gwen sat down in her white housecoat. "So the Krotch boys are trying to make people forget about their connection to Richardson by going after Sam and branding Milo as the kingpin."

Jean added cream to her coffee, taking a sip. "Can the kids hear us?"

Gwen leaned back in her chair, looking into the living room. The faces of the three boys were lit by the images on the TV. *How to Train Your Dragon 2* was playing, and all three appeared focused. "They're into the movie."

Jean said, "Maybe I should have told you before, but there is more to the video of Rod and the calf."

Gwen asked, "What's that got to do with Sam?"

Jean took another sip. "Nothing, but it could easily destroy the credibility of the Krotch boys."

"Can we see it?" Sydney asked.

Jean leaned over, reaching into her voluminous blue leather purse, pulling out a laptop. She set it on the table, putting her hand on the cover. "You may not want to see this."

Gwen's eyebrows met along the vertical line running above her nose. "There's not much I haven't seen."

Sydney shook her head. "What's on it?"

Jean opened the laptop, logging in, clicking an icon. "We have to think about this." Sydney and Gwen leaned in close to watch the entire fifteen-minute video.

Gwen sat back. "We need to get this out there right away!"

Jean said, "Not just yet. I know you want to nail them after what they did to you." She reached into a manila folder. "I also found this."

Sydney took the sheet and read. "We're almost there. We have to remember the Krotch boys are masters at diverting attention and evading answers to uncomfortable questions. The evidence will have to be overwhelming so their lawyers and their money won't allow them to slither out of this. If we take our time and build a solid case, there won't be even the smallest crack for them to get through."

Jean nodded. "And I was thinking about talking with my quilter friends." She turned to Gwen. "How would you feel about doing some interviews?"

. . . .

Doug Brown knocked on Giles Patriot's front door with his right hand. In his left he held a bottle of Fortaleza tequila. There was a thump inside, then the sound of a chair being pushed back, followed by footsteps. The door opened. Patriot stood there wearing a royal blue housecoat. There was a coffee cup in his left hand. His hair was washed and combed, his grey eyes clear and focused. He looked at the tequila then at

Brown. "What do you want?"

"The Brothers sent me to talk with you about a development." Doug made it sound like an order, because it was.

Patriot turned, walking down the hallway of his bungalow into the kitchen. "You'd better come in then."

Brown left his handmade alligator boots on but did wipe them on the floor mat before making his way to the kitchen.

Patriot poured himself a coffee, lifting the pot in Brown's general direction. "If you want some, get yourself a cup."

Brown found a cup in the cupboard above the coffee machine. He also spotted a couple of glass tumblers. He set the bottle and cup with the tumblers on the table, sitting down while Patriot poured the coffee. He turned, put the carafe back on its hotplate, sitting across from Brown.

Brown said, "Three guys from the Patriot Institute are coming to town."

"The three wise men?" Patriot added cream and sugar to his coffee.

Doug ignored the sarcasm while looking around the kitchen. The green drapes were closed, the dark green walls washed thin to olive in spots, the tiled counter top cleared of everything save a coffee maker and toaster. He guessed the cupboards were original to the fifty-year-old house. "The bosses wish to reestablish their local income stream. Corporation was their hub under Richardson so they're sending in the triplets."

Patriot used the open space between his thumb and forefinger to stroke his double chin. "And you will facilitate the operation."

Brown nodded, sipping his coffee, twisting open the cap on the tequila then pouring them each three fingers of blue agave.

Patriot looked away from the glass Brown slid toward him.

Instead, he stuck the coffee under his nose. "What's my end?"

"You welcome the triplets to town, introduce them on your show, talk about the Patriot Institute, let them talk religion." Brown reached for his glass and sipped. "This stuff is better than the best Scotch in my opinion."

"And my cut?" Patriot sipped his coffee.

"Two percent above the old rate of three."

"Five percent." Patriot set down his coffee, reaching for the tequila, sniffing, closing his eyes, tipping the liquid down his throat. He set the glass down, reaching for the bottle. "I want a better deal this time around. It's time for me to retire."

. . . .

Garrett and Fatima walked side by side, crossing Fourteenth Street on the way to Hexagon for a cup of coffee. The Sunday traffic was light under blue/grey skies. A raindrop hit the top of Garrett's head. He wiped at it, looking up.

Fatima asked, "You feel that?"

Garrett nodded, trying to keep up as she picked up the pace.

By the time they walked the three blocks to Hexagon, the individual spots of rain on the cement were joining together to create a shiny wet coat. Garrett inhaled the fresh scent of spring rain while climbing the steps and opening the door to Hexagon for Fatima.

Inside there was musty heat. Conversation ebbed and flowed around board games. Garrett joined a lineup for coffee. Fatima said, "I'll get us a table."

After five minutes of watching and waiting behind a couple who read the entire menu, asking questions about each item, Garrett ordered. He sat down with Fatima at a table next to the window looking down onto a dripping Kensington Road where dandelion umbrellas sprouted over concrete. Fatima had her purple fleece drying on the back of her chair. She looked to her right at a foursome playing Jenga.

The barista said, "Garrett!" He stood up, walking to the greenish blonde barista behind the espresso machine, and picking up two cups. He maneuvered his way back to the table. Fatima took her London fog. Her phone rang. She reached into her blue leather purse, pulling out the phone, and putting it against her ear.

Garrett sipped, watching her face. His phone rang. He picked it out of his shirt pocket. "Hello?"

"It's Sam."

"What's up?" Garrett watched Fatima's eyes turn a dangerous shade of violet.

Sam said, "Jean called. She has an idea for some more videos with Gwen Chorny and Jean's quilter friends. You available?"

Fatima wiped tears from her cheeks with her fingertips. He reached out, but she shook her head.

Sam asked, "You still there?"

"Something's happened to Fatima. Can I call you back?"

"Of course." Sam hung up.

Fatima said, "Okay," hanging up. She looked at her phone, and then at Garrett. "Laura just quit as the wedding planner. She says she doesn't want to stay on the medication, and I pressured her into being a planner. And she thinks it's unfair that we aren't paying her."

"But she convinced you to let her do the job. Said it was a wedding gift. That she didn't want to be paid."

Fatima shook her head, wiping some more tears away. "That's what she said. She also said she's looking for a new hair stylist."

"That's a relief."

Fatima nodded, smiling, and sobbing. "She told me she booked the reception but never did. The wedding's fucked up."

Later that evening, Garrett called Sam after Fatima went home. He dialed, sitting back, looking out the window. The sky was still grey. He looked at the ceiling. Grey again.

Sam asked, "How's Fatima doing?"

"Pretty upset. She was told the hall was booked, the church was booked, the caterer was booked, even the JP was booked. Now we find out none of it was done."

"Shit. That sucks."

Garrett shook his head. "How about you? The Krotch boys dream up any new bullshit to smear you with?"

"Not so far. Jean has a plan to deal with the drug kingpin lie. She and the quilters want to be interviewed by Gwen Chorny and you. Luke will do the camera work, then the videos will be uploaded on YouTube."

"Okay."

"So I'm asking if you would be willing to do some more videos."

"Okay."

"You don't sound okay."

Garrett leaned forward, putting his forehead in the palm of his free hand. "I'm just pissed over this wedding mess. Fatima is really upset. When do you need me?"

"Would Wednesday at Woody's around ten AM work?"

"I'll be there."

Sam said, "Thanks. Do you want me to see if the church is available for you and Fatima?"

"That would be nice. Then I'll run it by her. Things have gotten a little complicated around here."

"You all right?"

Garrett lifted his head. "I think so. See you Wednesday."

EIGHTEEN

<u>Wednesday, June 4</u>

0

The sun teased the cool from the morning air. Garrett sat next to Ella who was blue lipped from eating berries.

He looked across the lake to the Corporation cemetery where his grandfather was buried. All of the trees bordering the headstones were wearing a deeper shade of evergreen. He smiled at the memory of his grandfather's silver hair under the porch light of the farmhouse. His bear-sized paw dwarfing five-year-old Garrett's in a handshake.

Luke said, "We're ready over here."

Garrett looked over his shoulder to where Gwen Chorny sat in a lawn chair. She wore a light green, tailor made jacket. To her left was a woman on the far side of sixty. Her recently permed red hair was cut above the ears, and she wore a red blouse and skirt. Sam and Riley both wore their prairie dinner jackets and came over to keep an eye on Ella. She sat on a purple Mexican blanket. Ella watched Garrett standing in between the two women. He wore the blue shirt and black pants Fatima had picked out for him. She'd said, "It'll show off your eyes." He smiled at the two other women, handing his phone to Riley. Luke fixed a black microphone to the front of Garrett's shirt then moved behind the camera.

Gwen shifted her shoulders back, nodding. "Today we are talking with Mary Ruryk and Garrett MacGregor. Both have connections to Corporation, Alberta and have come out in support of the Sausage Festival planned for this coming Canada Day."

Mary nodded, looking at the camera, opening her mouth. Her whitened teeth glittered. "I think the Krotch brothers accusations against Sam Sieben are pretty despicable."

Gwen blinked. Garrett smiled, because Mary hadn't rhymed Krotch with couch. Luke kept focused behind the camera.

Gwen recovered. "You're referring to a recent editorial in the Upper Canada Press accusing Sam of plotting to take over former Mayor Richardson's alleged drug operation?"

Mary rolled her eyes. "Everyone knew Rod and his gang were selling drugs. I'm here to say that Sam did supply us with marijuana after we got the breast cancer." She leaned forward, looking at Gwen. "Did you know his mom, Rita, died of breast cancer? Did you know he took care of her during her last year? Did you know he grew a specific kind of plant to help with the chemo?"

Gwen asked, "Aren't you afraid you might face legal problems because of what you're telling us?"

Mary laughed. "I'm sixty-eight years old. What are they going to do? Arrest me! Yes, I'm guilty of putting marijuana in my muffins, cookies, and squares. You're damned right I did it, because it helped my friends who were going through chemo. And then when I had my cancer and double mastectomy–" She made a swiping motion across her chest. "– my friends did the same for me to help relieve the symptoms. It helped me sleep. Sam took a big risk in growing the stuff for us. And he's loved by most of the women in the community, because he never accepted a dime for what he did."

Gwen looked at the camera. "We haven't heard from you

Mr. MacGregor."

Garrett watched the way the breeze was working the surface of the lake. He turned to face Gwen. "It's a healthy way to deal with grief and tragedy."

Gwen's eyebrows lifted. "Can you clarify?"

Garrett shrugged. "This town experienced tragedy. Sam, Mary, Riley, and I think the town needs something to celebrate."

Gwen leaned a bit closer. "Some critics say a Sausage Festival is the wrong way to go about it."

He shook his head. "Most of those critics come from outside of the town." He looked at Mary. "So do you listen to the critics or do you listen to Mary?" He glanced over at Riley who was reading a text message. His eyes lifted and Garrett read his cousin's expression. "What's happened?"

Riley said, "It's Jacolynne. David's been in an accident."

. . . .

It took about an hour and fifteen minutes to make it to the Foothills Medical Centre. Ella started crying about half way there. Garrett found she would stop if he kept massaging her left foot. So he drove south the last hundred kilometres into the Foothills Medical Centre parking lot, all the while rubbing the sole of her foot with his thumb. They headed for emergency, walking past a clutch of smokers gathered outside–some in wheel chairs and some attached to IV poles or oxygen–then through the automatic glass doors where he spotted Fatima who held out her arms.

"He's banged up, but he's okay." She looked over her shoulder to the glass box insulating nurses from patients. "He's back there with Jacolynne and Dayna. It's on the right." She hugged them both.

"What happened?" He pulled the diaper from his pocket. "I need to change Ella."

Fatima put her hand on his cheek. "David slowed down for a construction zone. The pickup behind him was speeding and rear ended David. The rest is a blur."

She took hold of Ella in one hand, and the diaper in the other. "I'll take care of this, you go."

He kissed Ella on the cheek, walking past the nursing station, down the hall, searching for a friendly face. He spotted Dayna who waved him over and hugged him. Garrett took a long slow breath. She said, "He's okay. They just took some more x-rays and are waiting for the doctor to take another look." She took his elbow, leading him into a room where David lay on a bed guarded by his sister. She hugged her father, weeping until Garrett felt the tears through his shirt. David grimaced as he tried to turn his head with his neck in a blue brace. His close-cropped hair was stained with dried blood and speckled with dirt. Garrett leaned over him, seeing the cast on his left forearm. "What happened to your arm?"

David smiled. "Broken."

Garrett looked at Jacolynne. "How bad?"

"The doctor says he was lucky. It'll be six weeks in a cast."

David said, "Sorry about the Jeep dad."

Garrett tried to talk, found it wasn't possible, so he shrugged.

• • • • • • • • • • • • • • •

Garrett's phone rang on the drive home from the hospital. He pressed the button on the steering wheel. "Hello?"

"How's David?"

"Sorry, Riley, I was supposed to call. He's okay. They took x-rays. A broken arm, bruised, and banged up."

"That is very good news."

"Yes." An arcing wave of emotion rolled up, falling on top of him. Garrett pulled over to the side of the road, stopping, sobbing.

When he was done, Riley asked, "Better?"

Garrett choked out a sound somewhere between a croak and guffaw.

"I have good news about the church. Call me back." Riley hung up.

NINETEEN

<u>Sunday, June 8</u>

O

Fatima sipped her London fog, breaking off a piece of date square, and smiling. "Don't worry, they're just late. Besides, Ella probably needed some extra hugs because her daddy's got a day off." They sat at the big wooden kitchen table in Weed's Café. Around them sat groups of coffee drinkers, and two people drinking water, while tapping laptop keyboards.

Garrett sat with his back to the half wall. Fatima was on his left. She looked right through the doorway into the next room with the turquoise wall where more people sat and chatted. "Shit!" She put her hand on his forearm before he could turn around. "Don't look. Melissa is here with some guy." He felt his abdominal muscles contract.

He watched through the window, out onto the patio. Mark and Jacolynne pulled up in their grey Volkswagen SUV. Mark got out, releasing Ella from her car seat. She tucked her arm in around his as they headed inside, Jacolynne following. They stepped through the front door, Jacolynne smiling at her father, then frowning. Garrett had seen the expression before when Jacolynne was twelve. A neighbourhood kid was tormenting her brother. She took care of business with a hockey stick. She pushed her black hair back while Ella checked out the

Nanaimo bars and banana bread behind the glass display case.

Mark nodded at Garrett. Mark's eyes narrowed when his wife made her way around the half wall, through the doorway to the turquoise room. Fatima turned to Garrett. "Better go after her." She followed. He glimpsed the startled look on the face of the young woman behind the counter. "Hurry!" Fatima said.

Jacolynne's spine was razor straight. Garrett got a glimpse of Melissa. Her open eyes and mouth. The brown bob of her skull-hugging hair, the back of a blond man's head turning to see the approaching threat. Mark stood in the doorway blocking Garrett's view. Jacolynne said, "Hello Melissa."

Melissa forced a smile. "How are you?"

Jacolynne moved around the table to stand to one side of Melissa. Mark slipped around the other side of the table.

Don't get Ella in the middle of this! She might get hurt. Garrett stood behind the blond man sitting across from Melissa. She looked at Mark then back at Jacolynne. Melissa said, "This is my friend Roland."

Jacolynne leaned her head to the right. "How's the cheating and lying going?"

Garrett watched Ella who was looking down at the table and swinging her left leg back and forth. He looked at Melissa's coffee cup, seeing Ella's eyes focusing. Ella!

Roland began to stand with his palms facing the ceiling. "All's fair in love and war!"

Ella's toe caught the lip of Melissa's coffee cup. It tipped. A wave of steaming coffee rolled over the edge of the table onto her lap. She stood, knocking the chair back against the wall. "Shit!"

Jacolynne looked at the table, picking up a nearby napkin, handing it to Melissa while looking at Roland. "All's fair." Then she turned, walking around the table, looking at her father, and saying, "She won't be havin' any fun for a week or two." Mark followed her through the coffee shop and outside onto the deck.

Garrett moved over to the left as Roland walked Melissa out into the sunshine. There was a darker triangular patch of coffee brown on the white of her slacks. She glared at innocent Ella who was tucked up against David.

Roland pushed fingers through his blond mane. "You'd better do something with that kid. She's a freak!"

Ella pointed back. "Shit on you!"

Jacolynne said, "Ella!" Fatima laughed, followed by Garrett and Mark. Then came more laughter from the woman in the red blouse and those at her table. Garrett thought, *That's the first time Ella pronounced `sh'.*

. . . .

West of Weeds, at a steak house called Angus, Doug Brown sat in a booth with the Decker triplets. Robbie, Preston, and Steve were all black haired, weighing at or over two hundred pounds, with round faces and brown eyes. Steve was clean-shaven with short hair while the others wore beards and ponytails.

The waiters arrived. Their shirts and pants were black to match the décor; black leather and dark walnut. Plates were set before them. T-bone steaks, potatoes, and gravy for Robbie and Preston. A Caesar salad for Steve. Brown put the napkin on his lap, waiting until the triplets had their mouths full. "They want you guys in Corporation."

Preston looked up. He shifted a tennis ball of beef into his right cheek. "To do what?"

"Who's they?" Robbie asked.

The other three looked at him like he'd just pulled his dick out in the middle of O'Canada at the Stampede grandstand show. He blushed, cutting another chunk of his steak, sticking it in his mouth, and chewing.

Preston asked, "Do we commute?"

Brown cut a slice from his sirloin. "You'll live in Richardson's old place on Corporation Lake. It's over eight thousand square feet."

Robbie asked, "With Mrs. Richardson?"

Brown shook his head. They all knew the former Miss Stampede was still a model. "She's left for their house in La Jolla."

Robbie asked, "La who ya?"

Steve shook his head. "It's in California, near San Diego. Prime real estate."

Preston chewed and swallowed. "What's our end?"

Brown put his hand over his mouth. "You three take over the production and distribution side. You get a percentage."

Robbie sawed at his steak. "Who will be handling the retail side?"

Brown sliced another sliver of sirloin. "Not your concern. Your share will be bigger than Richardson's. He was averaging twenty-five million a year."

Steve said, "He's dead."

Preston looked beyond the booth. They were at least five metres away from a group of men in golf shirts who were drinking pitchers and talking louder by the beer.

Preston asked, "Not our concern?"

Robbie pointed his fork at his surroundings. "This place is one of our customers."

Steve said, "They pay for protection."

Brown shook his head. "This is small time stuff. They want you in Corporation tomorrow. You will be running the Richardson properties and posing as newly minted born agains."

Robbie smiled. "We know the evangelical routine."

TWENTY

<u>Monday, June 9</u>

*O*t her Corporation gas station, Shelly read the *Upper Canada Press* online. She leaned back, smiling. "Finally, not one story about our town." She looked up, spotting a red Dodge Ram diesel dual-wheeled pickup pulling up at the pumps, towing a red and white cargo trailer. There were union jacks on the rear fenders of the truck. She looked closer at the tailgate of the Ram as it turned. *CHRISTLER* was written in white letters against the red. The driver got out to fill the tank on the far side of the truck.

A man climbed out of the passenger door. He had a beard and a ponytail, wore a black leather jacket with an *IXOYE* badge on the front. She noted his black leather boots as he walked toward her kiosk. He opened the door, setting a hundred dollar bill on the counter, "Diesel for our pickup."

She took the bill, ringing it through the till, and handing him a receipt. "There you go."

He took the receipt then looked out the window. "We're looking for the Richardson place."

Shelly smiled, using her right hand to tuck her brown hair behind her ears. "Which one?"

Ponytail frowned.

Shelley fluttered her recently extended eyelashes. "The house or the acreage?"

"Uhh, the house."

"Take your next right, follow that road all the way to a T intersection, then turn left. It leads to the house. Biggest one on the lake."

The man nodded, then went out the door.

Shelly waited until both men were back in the truck before going to the door. As the pickup turned, she was able to memorize the plate. She went back behind the counter, picked up the phone and dialed. "Jean?"

"Shelly?"

"Yep. There are some new guys in town looking for the Richardson house. Have a pen handy? Got a plate number for you."

· · · · · · · · · · · · · · ·

Garrett was sitting in front of the TV, watching a rerun of Sherlock when the phone rang. He pressed pause and picked up the phone. "Hello."

"Hey Garrett, it's Riley. What are you doing on Wednesday?"

TWENTY-ONE

<u>Wednesday, June 11</u>

Garrett asked, "What are you building?" He and Ella stood outside of the open doors of Riley's red Quonset. It sat at one corner of the homestead yard. The yellow two-storey house was at another corner. Ella watched the chickens in the yard pecking at insects and small stones.

Riley took off his white dust mask. His grey shirt and pants were coated with sawdust. He looked at the wooden frame with the gentle arc. One by one inch stringers were glued and nailed to round forms. The banana-shaped spruce form lay on the concrete floor underneath a red high-winged home-built airplane hanging from the rafters. To one side was his rat rod made of a collection of car parts from domestic and foreign vehicles, creating a rusted masterpiece called Sheldon. "It's a little something for the festival." He looked at Ella, blushing. "A fifty foot erection." He turned back to the shaft. "I'm going to finish the frame today. The plan is to cover it with papier-mâché."

"Why not fiberglass?"

Riley winked. "The grande finale." He looked beyond Garrett. He turned to watch a blue Buick driving up the road between the north side of the house and the carragana hedge. Garrett picked up Ella when the car turned into the yard, parking beside his Ford. He saw three women in the Buick. He recognized Gwen Chorny wearing a blue jacket in the passenger seat. Jean was behind the wheel. A dark haired woman leaned to her left so she could see between the pair in the front seats.

Garrett asked, "Who is she?"

Riley waved. "Sydney Knox. She took Richardson down."

Garrett shifted Ella from his right arm to his left. She grabbed hold of his shirtsleeve.

The women climbed out. Sydney stood the tallest of the three as they moved into the Quonset.

Riley asked, "Coffee?"

Jean's eyebrows did a dance as she took in the sculpture. "Coffee would be nice."

Gwen asked, "What the hell is that thing?"

Ella said, "The grande finale."

Garrett smiled, rubbing Ella's back.

Sydney studied the toddler. "What's your name?"

Ella tucked her head in next to Garrett's. He said, "This is Ella."

Sydney reached out with her index finger, stroking the back of Ella's hand. Sydney turned to Garrett, smiling and said, "She's the brains of the operation, and she's what, two?"

Garrett nodded. "If I take her advice things usually turn out for the best."

They followed Riley to the far end of the Quonset where he had another homemade espresso machine made from a collection of parts in a variety of colours. The overall effect was neo-steampunk. It was next to a last century fridge.

Riley flipped a switch on the wall. The metal of his espresso machine began to hiss and click. He pointed at a couple of lawn chairs and some upturned plastic milk crates. "Have a seat."

Garrett chose a crate, watching Sydney wince as she eased herself into a lawn chair. She brushed her hair back. He saw the fading greens and purples on her forehead. Sydney looked back at him. "Ribs are slow to heal."

Ella squirmed on Garrett's knee. He looked around. At least one hundred sharp edges, and tools of varying levels of lethality made him hold Ella a bit tighter. The women looked at one another, wordlessly setting up a rough circle around a bare patch of concrete, smiling at Garrett. Gwen said, "Don't worry, we'll all keep an eye out for Ella."

Steam spat from the espresso machine. Riley asked, "Lattes all around?" He reached into the fridge for a jug of milk.

"Please." Gwen nodded.

Jean took Ella's hand when she squirmed off Garrett's knee, walked over, and took hold of the lawn chair. Jean asked, "Where's Sam?"

Riley soon handed lattes to Gwen and Jean. "On his way. He's checking in with Shelly and Luke. They're keeping an eye on both roads out of the Richardson place, just in case." He handed another cup to Sydney.

Garrett thought, *Every coffee shop should have one of these espresso machines. It can make six lattes at one time.* He took his cup from Riley who lifted his chin and smiled.

Riley sat down on an upturned crate with his own cup, turning as Sam walked into the Quonset holding a travel mug. He hugged the women in turn then hugged Garrett. "Thanks for being here."

Jean cupped her mug in her hands. "We'd best get started." She lifted her chin at Gwen.

Gwen looked around the circle. "We have been gathering bits of information and it's beginning to look like we have a complete picture." She reached into her bag for a laptop.

Sydney watched Ella who was walking the inner circle.

"There is a complication as well. The Decker triplets have moved into the Richardson house." She looked around. "You understand what I'm telling you is confidential? I'm not supposed to tell you, but you need to know for your own safety." She waited.

Sam and Riley looked at one another. Sam nodded, thumb and forefinger zippering his lips.

Garrett watched Sydney's brown eyes as he said, "I appreciate you telling us, actually. Please go on."

"The Deckers are Hells Angels. They spent time in prison for trafficking and possession. They had a job while they were inside." She watched Ella. "The Angels were paid to protect a couple of men convicted of sexually interfering with minors."

Sam looked like he'd just sipped sour milk. "You mean they were bodyguards for pedophiles?"

Sydney nodded. "That's correct."

Garrett stood up, reaching over, scooping up Ella. "How dangerous are these guys?"

Sydney shrugged. "They have no documented history of violence."

Jean said, "We have also been looking at connections between the Krotch brothers, Richardson, Giles Patriot, Doug Brown, and K&K Realty in Calgary. K&K–in turn–is owned by Nova Bank. The Krotch brothers are majority share holders of Nova Bank."

Gwen looked at Garrett. "The Krotch brothers' bank laundered Richardson's drug money."

Sydney said, "Doug Brown is their fixer, and he is a psychopath."

Jean looked at Ella. "Now the Hells Angels are back in the picture."

Gwen said, "We're going to blow the whistle on these guys."

Sydney said, "There will be repercussions."

Garrett looked at Ella. She stood sumo pose, her cheeks were round half apples. "I need to change her."

A cell phone rang. Sam stretched out a leg, pulling the phone from his jeans pocket.

Garrett reached into the bag next to his chair, dug for a diaper, and some wipes. He stood up.

Sam said, "That was Shelly. The triplets are on the way."

Riley pointed at Jean. "Okay if you pull your car inside while I get the doors?" He looked at Garrett. "Okay if the ladies take Ella so that you, me, and Sam can meet the triplets? I don't want them knowing about this meeting."

Garrett set Ella down in the back seat of Riley's rat rod. He pulled off her tights. He heard Sydney on the phone. "Larry we need you right now." Jean's Buick started up and a few seconds later Garrett heard the overhead door closing.

He wiped Ella's bum, put on the new diaper, and pulled up her tights.

Gwen leaned on the fender. She held out her hands to Ella. "Will she come to me?"

Ella looked at Gwen. Garrett reached into Ella's bag, pulling out a bottle of milk, handing it to Gwen. Ella gave Garrett a sideways glance. Gwen held the bottle, waiting. Ella exhaled, allowing him to hand her to Gwen. Ella took the bottle, watching Garrett. He said, "I'll be just outside." He walked to the door next to the closed overhead, stepping outside with Riley.

Garrett looked at his grandfather's house and the chickens pecking the ground out front of the metal gate. The sound of an approaching vehicle caused the chickens to stop, their heads swivelling. The vehicle slowed. Garrett leaned against the rear hatch of his car. Riley crossed his arms, standing next to his cousin. A red pickup rattled up the driveway, pulling into the yard. Garrett saw the Union Jack on the fender over its dual rear tires. He watched the driver make a wide turn, parking facing the house. *CHRISTLER* was written on the tailgate. A silver scrotum dangled off the trailer hitch. The diesel engine wheezed then stopped. Three men climbed out of the cab. Garrett got a brief whiff of diesel fuel. The guy who closed the passenger door wore a beard, ponytail, and Union Jack T-shirt. There were tattoos running up each wrist, disappearing under sleeves.

The driver was another version of the passenger with a black and white Army of Christ T-shirt. They were followed by a slender, clean-shaven, shorthaired, brown-shirted version of the triad's genetic anomaly. The driver's voice was a wheel in need of axle grease. "Do you have a relationship with our lord and saviour?"

Riley lifted his chin, looking sideways at Garrett.

They caught you by surprise, but my gut is sending an air raid warning. Garrett leaned forward, taking a step toward the trio. "What are your names and what do you want?"

Brown shirt tapped the side of the pickup's box. A dog hopped out to stand next to him. It was eighty pounds of mixed breed with a predominance of German shepherd. It stood next to its master. The hair along its spine rose up like tufts of uncut grass.

"You're the Decker boys." Riley moved to stand beside his cousin.

Army of Christ took a couple of steps, extending his hand. "Word travels fast in Corporation. Name's Preston."

Garrett thought about crossing his arms, remembering he'd just finsished changing Ella's diaper, grinning, extending his hand, shaking Preston's. Riley did the same.

Preston looked over his shoulder. "This is my brother Robbie." He nodded. "And that's Steve." Brown shirt was motionless. "We're new in town. Thought we'd be neighbourly and introduce ourselves."

Keep your mouth shut. Garrett watched the dog, then began

studying Steve who, in turn, studied him.

Heads turned at the rumble of another vehicle approaching on the gravel road.

Robbie asked, "Is Brown coming too?"

Garrett caught the warning glare Preston sent his brother.

A white Explorer drove into the yard. It had an RCMP logo and a roof mounted light bar. It rolled up, parking alongside Steve and the dog. Steve reached into the truck box, pulling out a leash, attaching it to the dog's collar.

The officer stepped out of the Ford. "Hey Riley. How are things?"

Riley didn't move or speak.

Garrett asked, "Have you met Preston, Robbie, and Steve Decker?"

The officer was at least six feet four, taller than any of the Deckers. "Not yet. I'm Constable Sutherland. How are you fellows?" He walked around the front of the car, moving to stand in between the Deckers and Riley.

Preston smiled. "Just introducing ourselves. We're new in the neighbourhood."

Garrett kept his tone neutral. "So that's your euphemism for what this is."

Preston's whitened smile was set in concrete. "My brothers and I follow in the footsteps of Saint Paul. We're unashamed about being born again."

Riley found his voice. The volume started low, working its way up. "So you drove ten kilometers, past more than a dozen farms just to proselytize to a couple of gay guys?"

"Christ spent his time with sinners." Robbie held his hands up, palms together.

That faux smile is getting really annoying. Garrett went to open his mouth when there was a wail from inside the Quonset.

Robbie said, "Your granddaughter is calling."

Garrett's anger was the blue flame at the tip of a welding

torch. His fists came up. He stepped forward. Riley grabbed his right arm. Sutherland put a palm against Garrett's chest. The constable glanced at Riley whose cable wire muscles staked Garrett to the spot.

Sutherland turned to the Deckers. "Looks like you guys aren't welcome here."

Preston's smile was a light year away from the black holes of his pupils. "We fear our freedom of conscience and religion is being challenged."

Garrett felt his body humming with rage. He opened his mouth. The words coming out, deformed at birth. "Motherfuckingshiteatingassholes!"

Riley held him tighter. "I'm asking you guys to leave. You've upset my cousin."

Sutherland looked at the dog. It opened its mouth, revealing canines. The constable put his hand on the butt of his Glock.

Steve said, "Time to go." He opened the back door, snapping his fingers. "Conrad, hup!" The dog hopped into the rear seat of the truck.

Robbie pointed an index finger at Garrett. "See you later Garrett the Carrot." He turned, walking back to the truck.

Preston said, "May you find peace in Christ." He took a few backward steps, then walked alongside the truck, climbing in behind the wheel. The engine rattled to life. The exhaust pipe shat a cloud of black smoke. Riley pulled Garrett away from the coal cloud. Sutherland watched the Ram drive away. The cloud drifted north and into the carraganas.

Sutherland looked at Riley. "What the hell was that all about?"

Garrett said, "Intimidation."

Riley said, "Ya think?"

After a cup of coffee with Ella asleep in the crook of his right arm, Garrett felt it was safe to speak. "Ella can't come here anymore. I will come, but it's not safe for her." He looked at Gwen, Sydney, Sam, Jean, Riley, and Sutherland, realizing they did not have the luxury of choice. "I'm sorry."

Riley shrugged, rubbing his cousin's back.

Sam said, "Now, does everyone understand why we need a Sausage Festival?"

Sydney was the first to laugh.

TWENTY-TWO

Friday, June 13

0

Garrett pushed Ella's stroller along the sidewalk approaching Fatima's shop. He recognized Conrad. The Decker triplet's dog was in the middle of a pack of four men wearing dark leather and glossy black German WWII style motorcycle helmets. Each wore a black and white skull bandana covering nose and mouth. They spanned the width of the sidewalk from shop walls to curb.

Garrett adjusted Ella's diaper bag. She wore white sunglasses and chewed Cheerios.

The men in black crossed their arms. Conrad sat. The shortest of the four asked, "How's Ella this fine morning?"

Garrett recognized Marco's voice. He looked beyond the four, seeing the door to Fatima's salon open.

Ella pointed with a Cheerio. "Move, please."

Marco said, "In a minute, we have to talk to your *pappy*."

Garrett heard the sarcasm. "What do you want?"

Marco said, "Just wanted to remind you we know where you live." He pointed at Ella. "And we know where to find your family."

Garrett took a slow breath. *Keep your cool. You expected this, just breathe, and think. Their game is intimidation. They're travelling in a pack. It's a cowardly act.* "And?"

"And we want you to stay out of your relative's business," Marco said.

Ella pointed at the bandanas. "Halloween!"

Garrett asked, "What are the masks for?"

Ella said, "Zombies!"

Marco looked sideways at one of the ponytailed Decker brothers who said, "You just stay away from Corporation, and we'll leave you alone." Preston pointed at Ella.

"Tima!" Ella said.

Fatima's black, high-healed boots pronounced her arrival. She wore a black apron to cover her dress. She walked around to the front of the bikers. Her right hand reached up, pulling off Marco's mask. Robbie's was next. He tried to grab her hand and missed. She backed up to stand next to Garrett and Ella. "You guys got a problem?"

Preston's squeaky-wheel voice spoke from behind a mask. "No problem. Just a friendly warning."

"What exactly are we being warned about, Preston?" Garrett looked behind the four.

Preston shook his head. "If you don't know, you are dumber than I thought."

Garrett stood on his toes, acting as if expecting to see someone behind the quartet. "Where are Doug Brown and the Krotch boys?"

Robbie asked, "How do you know about them?"

The door of the salon opened. A woman boiled outside. She went straight for Marco, grabbing him by the earlobe.

Marco said, "Ow! Ma!" He bent sideways and was dragged off the sidewalk onto the road by a sixty something woman with tin foil in her hair and black Borat eyebrows.

"What are you doing to this baby girl?" Marco's mother Renatta Delevechio asked.

Marco tried to swat her hand away. A car squealed to a

halt. A horn blasted. "Ma! That hurts! We're just talking!"

Ma shook her free finger in his face, pulling him back to the sidewalk. "You and your tough friends better leave these people alone! Dayna loves this little girl. You are a better man than this!" She dropped her free hand, lifting her left foot, taking her sandal off. Ma began swatting Robbie first. Her next swing hit Preston's raised arm. "Vaffangulu!"

Ella tossed a Cheerio in the air. Conrad caught it and gulped. Ella reached for another.

Steve pulled the dog back. A pair of police officers in their blues stepped out of the flower shop on the corner.

Preston spotted them, turning, pointing at Garrett. "You've been warned." He retreated. His brothers followed. They headed for four Harleys. Conrad hopped into the one with the sidecar.

Marco tried to follow, but his mother still had him by the ear with her right hand and was smacking him with the sandal. Marco said, "Ma! Let go!"

The first bike started up. Ma swung at Preston as he passed. Then she swiped at Robbie who ducked, swerved, skidded, and recovered. She swung one more time at Steve. Conrad caught the sandal in his mouth, his ears flapping in the wind.

Ma dragged Marco over to the curb. "Bring back my shoe culo!"

Ella said, "Vaffangulu culo!"

Ma blushed, looking apologetically at Garrett. "Sorry."

Fatima put her hand to her mouth, laughing.

Marco said, "Ma, let go of my ear."

She dragged Marco to the door of Fatima's shop, waiting for him to open the door, then pulling him inside.

Fatima looked at the diaper bag. "Did you get it?"

He nodded, tapping the diaper bag as he knelt down next to Ella who kept eating Cheerios. "You okay?" Ella asked, smiling, picking up another Cheerio.

He looked up at Fatima. "You were right."

Fatima nodded, stretching her arms out and up, embracing the sun. "I told Marco's mom what's going on. She has her sources."

"She sure knows how to handle him."

Fatima smiled. "Ma's not afraid of anything." She let her arms fall, focusing on Garrett. "You didn't know Marco was a momma's boy?"

Ella said, "Nice puppy."

. . . .

Garrett used his laptop to answer FaceTime. Fatima sat next to him. Her perfume was a gentle honey scent, her hair brushing against his shoulder. Sydney and Riley appeared on the screen. Sydney smiled then asked, "How'd it go?"

Fatima leaned closer to Garrett. "Pretty much the way you said it would. The four of them showed up with the dog. They tried to intimidate Garrett with vague threats about Ella. Then Marco's mom came out, grabbed her son by the ear, and that was pretty much it."

Riley asked, "Marco's mom?"

Garrett said, "Yes, she was getting a perm, had tinfoil in her hair, and took them all on. Lost her sandal though."

Gwen's face appeared then disappeared. "Her sandal?"

Fatima set her glass down on the coffee table. "She smacked a couple of them with her shoe, then the dog grabbed it when–" She looked at Garrett. "–one of them drove away with the dog in a sidecar."

There was laughter, it sounded like Sydney, then it began to spread. Riley asked, "Did you get the video?"

Garrett shrugged. "Downloaded a copy onto the laptop. It looks okay to me. Do you want me to send it or is Luke coming to town tomorrow?"

Riley nodded. "I'm gonna drive him down in the morning."

Sydney moved to one side. Jean took her place in front of the camera. "We're trying to predict their next move. Does anyone in your family have dealings with the Nova bank?"

Garrett shook his head. "The kids are both with my bank. It's a credit union."

Fatima said, "My business and house are free and clear."

Sydney leaned in. "Garrett, does your building have security cameras?"

Garrett sat back. *Shit!* "Yes."

Sydney asked, "Fatima?"

She shook her head. "No."

Sydney combed fingers through her hair. "Is it okay if Luke and Riley install cameras tomorrow?"

Fatima leaned her elbows onto her knees. "What for?"

Sydney leaned her head to the right. "The Hells Angels–the triplets in particular–are persons of interest in an arson investigation."

Garrett took a long breath.

Sydney said, "We have to be prepared in case of escalation. Were the police there today?"

Garrett nodded. "Two officers came out and the Deckers left."

"Good." Sydney looked to her left. "Gwen wants to say something." Sydney moved over. Gwen took her place next to Riley.

Gwen asked, "How's your son?"

Garrett nodded and smiled. "He's good. Broken arm. It'll heal."

Riley said, "We thought we'd better warn you."

Fatima put her arm inside Garrett's. "You mean about the arson?"

Gwen shook her head. "We mean about everything. This will probably get messier before it's over. That puts you, and your family at risk. Corporation is pretty well united after Melvin's death. Brown and the Deckers are considered outsiders, and everyone's keeping an eye on them. Patriot is the town joke. He has a couple of drinking buddies but that's it. The problem is the Deckers and Brown are anonymous in Calgary. That makes you vulnerable."

Fatima said, "It's a little late for that. Besides, Renatta is on our side. She's got eyes and ears on her son and his friends. Garrett and I've been through something like this before. We both know we're in too deep to back out. The thing is we need someone to keep an eye on our kids and Ella."

Gwen looked to her left then back at the screen. "Sydney has that taken care of. Still, there's risk."

Garrett shrugged. "Can we start getting the videos up and then the evidence? We need to get everyone watching the Krotch brothers' gang. If the media is on their doorsteps, it's going to put them on the defensive instead of the other way around."

Jean appeared between Gwen and Riley. "If you're still in, then you need to know the whole plan."

Fatima looked at Garrett then said, "Okay. Let's hear it."

• • • • • • • • • • • • • • • •

Doug Brown sat in his black Chev four-by-four pickup with a lift kit and oversized radial XScream tires. He opened the door, looking down at the Decker boys who stood in the yard out front of Richardson's Quonset hut. Brown stroked his blonde moustache, set his boots on the rocker panel, waiting.

Preston held his helmet under his right arm. "What's the problem? Garrett and his girlfriend got the message."

Robbie was a bobble head doll nodding and rocking on his heals. "Marco went with us. Now they know we mean business."

Preston set his helmet on the seat of his Harley, crossing

his arms, his boots a metre apart. "We stopped the pair of them outside her shop. She looked real scared."

Brown looked over at Steve who was watching Conrad chasing gophers as they poked their heads up out of their dens. They whistled, the dog ran over, barking down the hole only to be whistled at from another direction. Brown said, "You aren't saying much."

Steve turned his head, looking up, making eye contact. "What my brothers said."

Brown lifted his chin. "We've got more work to do."

. . . .

"Mom wants to spend Monday with Ella." Jacolynne picked up the diaper bag, stuffing a package of wipes inside.

Garrett shrugged, recognizing the end of the year dog-tired teacher look in Jac's eyes. He turned to Ella who sat with her back to the couch, setting matching dots from the red and white dominoes against one another. *How does that kid stay so focused? Her attention span is longer than mine.*

"They're downtown in the Bow Valley Hotel and plan on looking for a place in Springbank. Mom wants to take Ella shopping on Monday. They're looking at houses this weekend."

Ella looked for a match for one of the last dominoes then flung it against the wall. "Vaffangulu culo!"

Jacolynne looked at her father. "Where did she learn that?"

"Bikers." Ella said.

Garrett blushed. "Marco and some bikers from Corporation showed up in front of Fatima's. She and Marco's mom took care of it."

"Bikers?" Jacolynne picked up her daughter.

"The police were there just in case." *Shit, you're making it sound even worse!*

"And Ella was there?" Jacolynne looked at her daughter for confirmation.

Garrett held his hands out. "You can see the video. Nothing happened."

Jacolynne turned to her father, rolling her eyes. "I don't want her in the middle of your mess!" She grabbed the diaper bag and stepped out the door. Ella waved goodbye to her grandfather.

. . . .

Garrett was just rolling into bed when the phone rang. He read the caller ID and lifted the receiver. "Hi Jac, what's up?"

"It's me, Mark."

Garrett heard the uneasiness in his son-in-law's tone. "Everybody okay?"

"We're fine. Jac wanted me to let you know that Marie will take care of Ella next week so you can have a break."

Garrett inhaled. *The babysitter's been fired.* The thought of next week without Ella made him want to weep.

"Marie hasn't seen much of her and, well, Marie and Jac thought it would be good for both of them."

Garrett waited. *And Jac doesn't want Ella around me with this Corporation mess.*

"You there?"

"Yes."

Mark asked, "You okay with this?"

Garrett looked at the phone, pressing end.

143

TWENTY-THREE

<u>Saturday, June 14</u>

O

Luke put his hands behind his head, leaning back, watching the video on his laptop. His black hair was trimmed short, and his smile reached his brown eyes. He glanced at Garrett.

"These guys never learn." He looked at Riley who sat across the table, slurping a latte. "Okay if I upload it?"

Riley looked at Sam who said, "Jean said they agreed we should go with it if it's good."

Luke put his hands in the air. "This isn't good, it's fuckin' awesome. Two of the guys are recognizable. The old lady makes them look ridiculous and even though Preston's wearing a mask, his voice gives him away."

Riley leaned against the counter. "Okay by me."

Sam nodded. "Go ahead."

They looked at Garrett who shrugged. "Why not?"

Riley asked, "What's up?"

Marie is back in town, I screwed up, Jac is pissed at me for it, and it feels like I'm back where I was three years ago when I was living in a fog and sleeping on the floor of my old house. "Fatima was hoping you guys could put those security cameras up today, please."

Riley opened his mouth. Sam put his hand on his partner's shoulder. Riley closed his mouth.

Luke pointed at his laptop. "The upload will take a few minutes." He stood up. "Can you take me to Fatima's so I can check the lay of the land?"

. . . .

Garrett heard the key enter the door lock. He turned as Fatima opened the door. She had a cardboard coffee tray in her free hand. He took his feet off the coffee table, setting the remote down, standing. "Hi."

She shut the door, setting the tray on the counter. Her eyes were on him the entire time. "The boys just finished installing the security cameras."

"That's good."

She twisted one cup up and out of the tray's grip. "They said you weren't yourself." She sipped from the cup, crossing her free hand across her belly then leaning back against the counter.

Garrett circled to the opposite side of the counter, pulling the second cup out.

Fatima turned. "So, what is wrong with you?"

Garrett shrugged, sipping the coffee. It tasted of chocolate scraped from the floor of a gas station bathroom.

"I talked with Jac, you know."

Shit. He took another sip, burning his tongue.

"Said she asked Marie to look after Ella next week."

He nodded.

"She said it upset her when Ella was in the middle of all those bikers."

He shrugged, setting the cup on the counter.

"You and I screwed up, and I told her that." Her eyes stayed on him, gauging his reaction.

Garrett lifted his eyebrows.

"She said Marie has been guilt tripping her into spending more time with Ella."

He inhaled and exhaled, feeling more than twenty years of ex on his chest.

"Jac sounded guilty and a little worried. She said her mom and Fergus deserve a second chance. It sounded to me like she was trying to convince herself." Fatima freed her index finger from the coffee cup, pointing it at him. He focused on the red fingernail. "It was you who raised those kids while Marie pursued her career." She raised her eyebrows to make sure he heard the sarcasm injected into the word 'pursued'.

He looked out the window at the afternoon sun and the green on the treetops.

"Then Jac started talking about how you had made all of her baseball games and David's football games, and how you'd always been at parent teacher interviews. That when they were in their teens you were always home. It was a weird conversation, like she was apologizing for over-reacting, but couldn't admit it."

Garrett said, "For the last couple of hours I've been back."

"Where?"

"Back in–" He used his free hand to explode the fingers near his ear. "–side the place I used to live. Where I lived before I met Dayna and you."

She leaned her head to the right.

"Want to go out for dinner?"

Fatima nodded. "I think that's a good idea."

. . . .

Robbie turned around to check if the plastic crate in the box of the pickup was sliding around.

Preston glanced right at his brother. "Stop fuckin' worrying. You put four bungie cords around that thing."

"Just checkin'."

Preston eased back on the accelerator, turning up the music. Celine Dion sang about the power of lurv.

"What's lurv?"

Preston tapped his left boot on the floor. "Whad'ya mean?"

"She said 'lurv' man." He pointed at the radio.

They drove into the shade under the overpass running west to Airdrie. "That's just the way Celine sings. Get over it."

Robbie looked west where the sun was sitting on the tips of the Rockies. "How come Steve stayed home?"

"His dog was sick."

"I'm hungry. How 'bout we stop at Bob's for a burger?"

• • • • • • • • • • • • • • •

Garrett opened his eyes. The clock indicated two AM. Fatima snored. He closed his eyes. The chocolate cheesecake after the pizza lounged heavy in his belly. Slow release caffeine made his nerve ends dance. He exhaled, rolling off the mattress. *Go for a walk. Maybe that will help.*

Ten minutes later, he stepped out of the condo's front door, turning north.

• • • • • • • • • • • • • • •

Robbie chewed a cold French fry. "Now?"

Preston opened his door. "Yep." His boot heals clapped the pavement. They parked a half block north of Fatima's in front of a lawyer's brown-stuccoed office. Preston looked south along the alleyway behind a row of small businesses then turned to close his door.

• • • • • • • • • • • • • • •

Garrett did a circuit around the Queen Mary schoolyard, an oasis of playing fields and mature trees across the river from the centre of town. He'd spent fifteen years teaching at the high school. The shrubs set in front of the brick cast blackout shadows. He remembered an email from the elementary principal. "Please stop your students from copulating out front of my office window."

Another fifty metres, and he turned right to cross the street. Ahead was a house with river-stone walls and a polished copper front door. His feet and a single vehicle on 19th Street made the only sounds. He stopped at the corner. A red dodge pickup was parked back from the street light near the lawyer's office. The word *CHRISTLER* was painted on its tailgate. Garrett walked up to the truck, peering in the box. In the shadow of the back corner sat an empty crate. He looked up and down the alley. A figure moved past the Dumpster across the street from his condo.

He crossed the street and into the alley. Power poles, Dumpsters, and parked cars were his cover. Garrett stood behind a Dumpster half way down the alley, looking over top. Two people of uniform height stood on the pavement behind the coffee shop. There was the clink of glass. One said, "This is it."

The other pointed at Fatima's back door. "No, it's that one." His voice was pitched higher.

A lighter flickered. One wick, then another painted the pair with yellow light. Both wore balaclavas.

Garrett looked down, seeing the light from above the door of the flower shop sending his shadow across the alley. He moved up against the Dumpster. His nostrils filled with earthy tones of decomposing vegetation.

High-pitched voice said, "Careful!"

That's Preston!

The other said, "I'll get this one. You get that one!"

Sounds like Robbie.

"No!" Preston tried too late to grab his brother's arm. The Molotov cocktail arced a glowing tail, shattering and splashing fire against the back wall of the coffee shop. Both men were illuminated. "Not there." Preston grabbed Robbie's elbow as his brother picked up another cocktail.

Robbie pulled away. The bottle slipped. Preston fumbled for it. Garrett heard the pop when the bottle hit the pavement. A pool of spreading fire surrounded Preston's boots. Robbie dodged back, knocking the remaining bottles over. Preston raised his knees, dancing in the pool of fire. One boot's leather sole slipped on a patch of gravel. Preston's ass hit the fire. Then he was up and running toward Garrett. His boots clumped on the pavement, feet and backside on fire.

Robbie ran after. "Stop, drop, and roll!"

Preston ran past Garrett. He was trying to outrun the fire licking the back of his pants. He ran across the street. Robbie followed, tackling his brother on the grass in front of the lawyer's office.

Garrett caught the stink of burnt gasoline and flesh. He sneezed, reaching for his phone. When he looked up, Preston was sitting on the grass, yelping, arms out front, knees bent, dragging his backside, planting his heels, lifting them, repeating the process. He was at the centre of a cloud of smoke. Preston howled, "My ass!" He rolled, shoving his brother away. "Find a fucking hose!"

Garrett looked over his shoulder. The back wall of the coffee shop was lit. He looked back at his phone and dialed 911. He heard the connection open then said, "A fire at Hillhurst Coffee on 19th Street!"

He looked at the fire, then to the Ram pickup. The driver's door slammed. The starter whirred, then the clatter of a diesel engine, followed by a wheezing turbo. The truck accelerated east, leaving behind a black cloud to mix with the white smoke hanging above the grass.

Ten minutes later, the alley was red, white, and blue from emergency vehicles. The pumper's diesel pushed away the quiet as firefighters in yellow aimed water at the fire. The roof went concave, collapsing, the fire climbing and illuminating the wall of Garrett's condo.

He sat in the front seat of a black and white police cruiser rereading his witness statement.

"What the fuck?"

Garrett looked right. Fatima had her right hand on the door. She wore an untucked white blouse and white pajama bottoms. He said, "I couldn't sleep and went for a walk."

She looked over the roof of the car. "Who did this?"

"Preston and Robbie Decker. They threw Molotov cocktails."

"Why the coffee shop?"

"They argued over which shop was yours and got it wrong."

Fatima looked at the witness statement in his hands. "How do you know it was them?"

"I heard their voices and recognized their truck." He pointed at a police officer directing traffic. "He told me my story checked out. Two guys are in custody at FMC Emergency."

"Think they'll be able to save my shop?"

"You don't sound all that upset?" Garrett set the witness statement on the dash, pulling himself up, and out of the car, putting his arm around her shoulders. He felt her shrug and fought off a smile.

"Shit happens. As long as the kids are okay, this can be fixed. I was thinking of remodelling anyway." She reached for the phone in his shirt pocket. "Did you phone the kids?"

"Let them sleep."

She lifted the phone. "We need to know if they're okay."

. . . .

YYC News
Arrests Made in Arson Case

Two suspects are in custody after an early morning fire destroyed Hillhurst Coffee and damaged a neighbouring hair salon. One of the accused is in custody at the Foothills Medical Centre. The other is being held at the Remand Centre.

Staff Sergeant Donna Rollins of the Calgary Police serious crimes unit said, "The two are being held in connection with the fire and will be charged later. Both are known to the police. Security cameras recorded the incident."

Rollins went on to say, "The witness confirmed the pair uttered threats earlier in the week, and the threats were recorded."

153

TWENTY-FOUR

Monday, June 16

*O*atima said, "There's nothing worth saving." She wore rubber boots in the ankle deep water where bottles and cans of hair products bobbed in the wake of her passing. The walls were soot covered, the chair covers melted, and mirrors cracked. They'd spent the afternoon waiting for permission before being allowed inside.

Garrett's phone rang. He checked the name, looked at Fatima, saw the tears, and raised his eyebrows.

"Better answer it." She pulled a tissue form her jeans pocket, dabbing her eyes.

Garrett pressed answer. "Hello Jac."

"Dad! We're at the mall. We can't find Ella. Can you come?"

The muscles around Garrett's heart contracted. His free hand slapped his sternum. "Where are you?"

"Customer service. The police are here."

Garrett looked at Fatima. He covered the phone and choked. "Ella's missing."

She flat palmed his back, shoving him toward the door. "Let's go!"

Five minutes later they were accelerating up Shaganappi

Trail. Fatima was behind the wheel. He glanced at the speedometer. One hundred and sixty! He looked right. For an instant he saw the red 'd' in the center of the Alberta Children's Hospital sign. A moment later his seat belt gripped him as Fatima hit the brakes to make the turn onto 32nd Avenue. The Ford was on the edge of a four-wheel skid. Fatima jammed a palm onto the horn when a black mini van thought about running a yield sign. He caught a glimpse of a bearded guy with a phone at his ear, then read the man's lips, "What the hell?"

Garrett had his left hand on the dash and his right on the door handle as Fatima took a hard right. She put her right palm on the horn, held it there, then rolled up onto the sidewalk, stopping next to a police cruiser. Garrett released his belt, climbing out the passenger side.

A police officer pointed at Garrett. "You can't park there."

Fatima slammed her door and pointed. "It's his granddaughter who's missing!"

The officer rolled her eyes, leaning her head to the right. "Go!"

Fatima held the door open, running behind Garrett who caught a whiff of coffee when he passed Starbucks. Their rubber boots clumped, telegraphing their flight. There were startled looks, sleeping toddlers, and near collisions with oblivious shopaholics. They arrived out of breath at customer service. Jacolynne was red eyed, standing next to a police officer who was talking into the radio at his shoulder. Jacolynne sagged into Garrett's embrace. *She's aged a decade.* He held her up when her knees gave way. One of the women at the desk rolled a wheelchair behind Jac.

Fatima asked, "What happened?"

Jac pointed at Marie who sat in a chair. Fergus sat across from her. A young police officer sat on the end table. Marie wore an elegant green blouse and white slacks. She tucked the right side of her bobbed hair behind her ear when the officer handed her a tissue. She smiled up at him. A collection of shopping bags surrounded her chair. Garrett counted eleven. He watched as she put her hand on the officer's, smiling up at him. Garrett looked at Fergus who sat with one leg crossed over another while checking his phone. "She was buying shoes over there–" Jac pointed to her left at Faldo's "–and Fergus was on the phone."

Garrett asked, "Where are David and Mark?"

Jac said, "David's searching the shops. Mark is on his way in from Okotoks." She looked past her father. "Thanks for being here."

Garrett turned. Dayna and Siobhan hugged Fatima. Dayna asked, "What can we do?"

Garrett looked at Fergus who had his eyes all over Dayna. Fear and rage swirled, narrowing, funnelling to a point. Garrett took a step toward his brother.

Fergus' eyebrows knitted themselves into a question. "What?"

Fatima grabbed Garrett's arm. "Not now."

She moved so he could see her face. Fatima took his cheeks between her hands. "We need to find Ella first, then I don't give a shit what you do to your brother."

Garrett looked at the police officer with the square jaw, blond hair, and blue eyes. "What can we do?"

The officer pulled away from Marie who gave Garrett the stink eye. Garrett read Alexander on the officer's nameplate. He said, "It's very hard to wait and let us do our jobs, but that's what I have to ask of you."

Fergus said, "Don't be a hero Garrett."

Garrett took a long breath. Dayna grabbed hold of his other arm. "We need to find Ella."

Fatima faced the officer. "We know Ella, and we're not going to sit here, so you have a choice."

Alexander looked around him, seeing there were no nearby uniforms. "The washrooms have been checked and all exits are covered. Uniforms are doing a store by store search."

Fatima pulled a phone from her pants pocket. She looked at Jacolynne whose hazel eyes were coming into focus. "You got yours?"

Jac reached into her pocket, lifting her phone.

Fatima looked at Garrett, Siobhan, and Dayna. "You've all got Jac's phone number right?"

Dayna nodded. "Siobhan and I will head that way." She pointed east.

Fatima took Garrett's elbow. "We'll go the other way." She pointed at Jac, holding her phone up. "We'll keep you in the loop."

Jac managed a smile.

They walked side by side. Garrett's eyes swept left to right. He searched for blonde hair and Ella's bouncing gait in every open door. They turned west. He felt his mind clearing as he got into the rhythm of the walk. He looked past the people ahead. He remembered Ella hiding behind a wall of bras in The Bay and her laughter. "I have an idea."

In three minutes they stood in front of a wall of red, black, white, and mauve bras. The word `TRIUMPH' was written in black on a white wall. Garrett thought, *We could use one of those right now.*

They began at one end of the wall. Garrett got down on his hands and knees to look for a tiny pair of feet. Fatima looked behind. Someone coughed. Garrett looked over his shoulder. A clerk had her arms crossed. Garrett sat back on his knees. The woman's nametag said Debbie. Fatima asked, "Have you seen a little girl?"

Garrett held his left hand above the carpet in an estimate of Ella height. "Year and a half, blonde hair, blue eyes?"

"Who are you?"

Garrett said. "Grandparents."

Debbie's eyes shifted from annoyance to concern. "I'm sorry, no. Can I help?"

"She hid on me behind the bras one day," Garrett said.

The trio systematically searched displays and behind counters. Debbie came to Garrett, holding out her hands, "Sorry, no luck."

Fatima said, "Thank you."

Garrett looked at his feet. "Do you think Steve Decker or Doug Brown had something to do with this?" *Is this my fault?*

Fatima took him by the elbow. "Let's get a cup of coffee. We need to think where she might be." She walked him out of The Bay and into the mall. They passed a cookie shop and outdoor clothing store.

He said, "Ella and I come here on cold winter days when we want a walk. We get a bag of popcorn and she runs. It's a good place for her to burn off some energy."

Fatima said nothing as she continued to scan doorways and shops.

"What a funny kid she is. She goes flat out, then falls asleep anywhere. I've seen her stop half way up stairs, curl up, and nod off."

They walked past the Monkey Palace where kids played on fiberglass cars, airplanes, bridges, motorcycles, and a locomotive. Fatima pulled him left toward Deville. Garrett stopped. He looked at Faldo's shoe boutique.

She tried to pull him along, stopping when she saw his wide eyes. "What?"

"Maybe." He turned back toward the Monkey Palace. Strollers, parents, and kids waited at the blue gate under the palm trees. He noticed the young woman tending the palace appeared to be seventeen. He'd not seen her there before. *She might not know about the hiding place.* He walked around and between the line up. "Excuse me, please."

A woman said, "Wait your turn!"

He reached down, sliding open the lock on the gate.

Someone said, "Hey! Take your shoes off!"

Garrett walked across the blue/grey sponge floor to the red fiberglass convertible with the white seats. A boy of two or three climbed out from behind the wheel, running for the black motorcycle. Garrett put his right hand on the windshield and his left on the fiberglass trunk. He bent over, looking under the dash. The car was hollow all the way to its grill. He saw a sparkling red running shoe. His eyes adjusted to the shadow. A mauve T-shirt and black leggings. The back of a blonde head. The gentle rattle of Ella's snoring. He sobbed, resting his left shoulder on the seats, reaching out with his right hand. He touched her shoulder, gripping her right bicep, pulling her back. He slid out of the car and onto his knees. He used both hands to pull her out, then he turned to look at Ella's face, her eyes closed as she slept. He held her close. She wrapped her right arm around one side of his neck then settled her head against the other. He held her there for a moment. He felt Fatima's fingers on his face, wiping his tears so he could see. Then she took out her phone and dialed.

Garrett stood, walked to the gate, and through a cluster of people. He went to his right, heading for customer service. He heard Fatima say, "We found her. We'll be there in a second."

There was a scream, evolving into a howl of relief. It bounced off the ceiling and skylights. Each person in earshot of the intersection of four hallways looked toward the sound as Garrett moved toward customer service. He saw Jac in her black jacket and yoga pants. She had her back to him. The woman at customer service pointed at Garrett. Jac turned. She began to run, tripped, and fell.

Thirty minutes later, Ella was on David's knee, Garrett was finishing a mocaccino, an EMT wrapped Jac's sprained wrist. Marie hugged her daughter around the shoulders. "So happy

Ella's safe. Sorry we have to run. We have an important dinner engagement."

Fergus waved a handful of packages from about two metres away. "Sorry, but we can't be late." He turned, walking east, throwing a comment over his shoulder, "That was fun." Marie carried a package in each hand and followed.

Ella watched them walk away. "Bye grandma."

Marie didn't hear. The clicking of her heels receded into the general hum of passersby.

Fatima said, "Come on. Meet at my place, and we'll order supper in. This was quite the day."

Jac sat in a chair, reaching for Fatima with her uninjured hand. "I'm sorry about your shop. Dayna told me it's a write off."

Fatima crouched, putting her hands on Jac's knees. "Ella is safe. It's all good."

Jac looked at her daughter, then at her father. "How did you know where to look?"

Garrett shrugged.

Dayna said, "He knows Ella."

TWENTY-FIVE

Tuesday, June 17

0

Upper Canada Press

Grandfather Seeks Insurance Payday

By Elizabeth Chevrolet

The lawyer for two men charged with arson in Calgary reports that Garrett MacGregor hired them.

Preston and Robert Decker are being represented by lawyer Conrad Lerant. Lerant said, "Both men told me they were hired by MacGregor to torch his fiancés hair dressing shop on Saturday, June 14."

The Decker brothers were arrested at the Foothills Medical Centre where Preston Decker was receiving treatment for burns.

Lerant went on to say that MacGregor's benevolent public persona is quite the opposite of his ruthless private character. "Fergus Macgregor (Garrett's brother) will testify that Garrett staged the disappearance of his granddaughter. The child was reported missing on Monday in a Calgary mall. Garrett MacGregor conveniently discovered the child after a massive search by police and mall security."

When contacted by UCP, Fergus MacGregor said, "The way Garrett exploits his grandchild is criminal."

Garrett Mcgregor refused to comment when contacted by UCP.

• • • • • • • • • • • • • • • • •

Garrett sipped his coffee while sitting on the couch and looking out the window. The front door swung open. Ella stood there dressed in pink tights and a long white shirt. Jac stood behind her. She smiled at her father. "Thanks for doing this on such short notice."

He smiled, pushing himself up off the couch. Ella dropped her pink backpack and ran to him. She asked, "Where's Tima?"

"Right here." Fatima walked into the room in her black T-shirt and sweatpants. She walked over, wrapping her arms around Ella and Garrett.

Jac asked, "Did you read the news article?"

Garrett looked at his daughter who said, "It's online."

Fatima turned, flipping open the lid of the laptop. "UCP?" She looked at Garrett.

He sat Ella in the high chair, put some Cheerios in a bowl, and set them in front of her. He reached into the fridge for a bowl of raspberries. She said, "Booberries?"

Garrett turned back to the fridge, fishing out a package of blueberries. He set them in front of Ella. She used her thumb and forefinger to pick them.

"Say thank you, Ella." Jacolynne reached for one of the raspberries.

"Hungry?" Garrett asked.

Jacolynne pulled a chair up next to her daughter. "I was in a rush this morning and skipped breakfast."

Garrett set some bananas on the kitchen table. Jac reached for one and began to peel.

"This is bullshit!" Fatima pointed at the laptop screen.

"Bullshit!" Ella said as she contemplated a raspberry.

Fatima blushed. "Sorry." She turned to Garrett. "You'd

better read this."

Garrett shrugged. "Already did."

Jacolynne chewed a bite of banana. "There's more. Mom phoned last night. Fergus got a job with Nova Bank in Toronto."

Fatima crossed her arms, looking at Garrett watching Jacolynne.

She blushed. "I'm sorry. I was mad at you. Now I've got you in a worse mess. I trusted mom and Fergus. I thought she had changed, that she wanted to spend time with Ella."

Ella nodded. "Fergus mean to me." She picked up a blueberry, putting it in her mouth.

Fatima said, "Fergus betrayed you for a job at Nova Bank."

Garrett shrugged.

Ella said, "Vaffangulu Fergus."

Jac said, "This is my fault."

Garrett shook his head. "Fergus and Marie suit each other. It's all about getting what they want."

Fatima touched Jac's arm. "Okay if we take Ella to Deva Darr's?"

Jac handed Ella a chunk of banana. "Who?"

"An old friend who runs a shop with wigs and boots and–" Fatima glanced at Ella "–other stuff."

Jac shook her head without comprehension. "Sure, why not?" She looked at the stove clock. "I've got to go." She kissed Ella on the cheek and left.

Garrett looked at blueberry face Ella, then at Fatima sipping coffee. "Deva Darr's?"

"Actually, it's Darr's sister Sanjiv we want to see. She's a lawyer. I just need to make a few phone calls first."

They pulled up out front of Deva Darr's around ten thirty that morning. The red brick building was south of the Bow River and the zoo. The old two-storey fire hall in Inglewood had been transformed into a boutique, salon, laser service, lash lounge, pedicure, manicure, body sugaring, and Sandhu Law. Garrett parked out front between a pickup and a sub compact. He got out, lifting Ella out of her seat. She wriggled her legs. "Down!" He set her onto the sidewalk. They followed hand in hand behind Fatima and through the door set between a pair of garage doors. Inside was one wall of wigs set on white and brown manniquin heads. Pink, purple, blue, and yellow wigs were on the top shelf.

Fatima was hugged by a thirty something dark haired, round-faced man with an immaculately trimmed beard and shaved head. He wore rings on every finger, neon green glitter nails, a black open necked shirt, and wide legged silk navy palazzo pants over stilettos. "Sorry to hear about your shop. Where am I gonna go for a cut and colour now, Fatima?"

Fatima tapped Darr's shoulder, turned and said, "Darr, this is Garrett and Ella."

Ella wrapped herself around Garrett's leg.

Darr put his hands on his hips. "So you're the guy she loves!" He hugged Garrett. "Be good to her, she's good people."

Garrett smiled as Darr knelt to get eye to eye with Ella who reached out to touch the silk of his pants. She smiled, touched his ringed right hand, and said, "Nice."

"Thank you doll." He lifted her up. "How about we take a tour?"

A pair of boots caught Garrett's eye. They were high-heeled, knee-high leather with bejeweled flowers. "These are amazing."

Darr covered Ella's ear. "They'll get you from the bathroom to the bed."

Ella pointed at Fatima. "Red!"

They looked at blushing Fatima who pointed at a door in the opposite wall. "Is Sanjiv in?"

Darr smiled. "Okay, I'll let you off without embarrassing

you any more." He pointed, walking toward an oak door with opaque glass set in the top half. Then he pointed at Garrett, setting Ella down. "Go after those Krotch brothers, they are nasty bastards." He grabbed his crotch with his right hand, turning his left thumb towards the ceiling, then flipping his wrist, thumb pointing to the floor. He opened the door.

Ella took Garrett's hand, and they followed Fatima who said, "Try not to stare." The walls were light grey and adorned with copies of Matisse and Frida Kahlo's Love Embrace.

The secretary sat behind a gothic, green-topped oak desk that might have been two centuries old. It gleamed with polish and a fresh clear coat. "Mr. MacGregor and Ms. Delvechio?"

Darr said, "And Ella!" He closed the door.

"And of course, Ella." The man with the white shirt, black tie, and blazer stood. His brown hair was combed back, his face was angular, and his shoulders narrow.

Garrett noticed the man's face was hairless with no evidence of an Adam's apple. His eyes were glacier blue; the one bit of colour in that black and white ensemble. KELLY was inlaid in white on a black desktop nameplate. Garrett pointed at himself. "Okay if you call me Garrett?"

Kelly smiled. "Of course. Ms. Sandhu will be right out. She's puking her guts out in the washroom. First trimester morning sickness."

Garrett opened his eyes wide.

Ella said, "Get you from the bathroom to the bed."

Kelly got up from behind the desk, walking around to the front. With a dancer's grace, he floated to kneeling, tilting his head to the left, offering a hand to Ella. "What do you think of Darr?"

Ella grabbed the crotch of her blue pants. "Nasty bastards."

Kelly smiled.

Fatima lifted Ella up. "Not a good idea, Ella."

Ella wrapped a strand of Fatima's hair around her finger.

"Bad idea?"

Fatima nodded, smiling.

A woman stepped out of the washroom shared with Darr's side of the building. She was six feet tall, wore a green blouse to match her eyes, black yoga pants, pumps, and shoulder length hair. Garrett noted the athletic grace in her walk. *She is stunning.*

Fatima elbowed him in the ribs.

He faced his fiancé. *I wasn't staring!*

Kelly said, "Sanjiv, this is Mr. MacGregor and Ms. Delvechio."

Sanjiv smiled, walking closer to face Ella. "And who is this?"

"Ella." She looked at Sanjiv's red glitter nails as she offered her hand. Ella touched the nails. "Red."

"How old is she?" Sanjiv looked at Fatima.

"We say she's two." Fatima nodded. "She's closer to a year and a half. It just makes things easier. Thank you for seeing us."

Sanjiv shook her head. "Darr speaks fondly of you." She hugged Fatima, released, then offered her hand to Garrett. "You wished to discuss a problem with the Krotch brothers."

Garrett nodded, shaking her hand. Her fingers gripped his. In that moment he knew, *This one is no push over.*

She led the way to her office set at the back of the larger room. She walked through the open door, indicating they should sit in chairs set around a maple table in front of a desk. It was the mate to Kelly's. The wooden chairs were of mixed parentage, restored to their former sturdy polished glory. Ella sat on Garrett's knee while eying a bowl of chocolates. Sanjiv asked, "Tea, coffee–" She glanced at Ella. "–or juice?"

Ella said, "Juice!"

Garrett looked at his granddaughter, raising his eyebrows.

Ella said, "Please."

Sanjiv turned, lifting her phone. "Could we please have–" She looked over her shoulder.

Fatima said, "Coffee please."

Garrett pointed at Ella. "One apple juice and a coffee please."

Sanjiv continued, "–one apple juice, two coffees, and one tea." She set the phone down, taking her time turning around. She put her right palm on her belly. "This little one is already causing problems." She glanced at the bathroom door.

Fatima put her hand on Sanjiv's arm. "What can we do?"

Sanjiv smiled. "Stop the floor from moving." She took a couple of slow breaths. "Okay. You wanted to see me about this morning's piece in the *Upper Canada Press*."

Garrett nodded. "I think it's called defamation."

"It is. What can you tell me about the Decker brothers?"

Ella leaned back against Garrett who said, "I couldn't sleep and was out for a walk the night they set the fire. They used Molotov cocktails to burn the coffee shop and Fatima's place, they argued, one of the Molotov coctails spilled, and one of the brothers, Preston I believe, was burned. They left in their truck and I called 911."

"They were later apprehended at the hospital?"

"Yes." Ella leaned to her right.

Garrett glanced at Ella. "She hears everything we talk about at home."

"The article states you paid Preston and Robert Decker to set the fire." Sanjiv lifted her chin when Kelly opened the door with a tray of cups, a pot of tea, and carafe of coffee. She slid the tray onto the table, handing the bottle of apple juice and a straw to Ella. "There you go."

Garrett and Fatima said, "Thank you," in stereo. Fatima leaned forward to add sugar and cream to her coffee while Garrett opened Ella's juice, putting the straw in. Sanjiv poured tea into a white china cup then set the pot down. "What context can you offer about your brother's remarks?"

Garrett shrugged. "We're not close. Fergus is the biological father of my daughter–"

Sanjiv sipped her tea, watching, and listening without comment.

"–and we just learned this morning he has a new job with Nova Bank in Toronto."

Sanjiv nodded, setting her cup down. "We will have to prove that Fergus, along with the Decker brothers, were offered incentives to defame you."

Fatima looked at Garrett. "Maybe Renatta Delvechio can help us there."

"Sydney can help." Ella said just before she took a sip of juice.

They all turned to look at Ella.

Sanjiv asked, "Who is Sydney?"

Garrett stirred milk into his coffee. "She's the RCMP officer who shot Rodney Richardson in that Corporation massacre. She and two others have been gathering information about Richardson, Brown, the Decker triplets, and the Krotch brothers."

Sanjiv asked, "Brown?"

Fatima said, "Doug Brown. He's a fixer for the Krotch brothers. Keeps the Krotch's at arms length from the dirty work."

Sanjiv looked at the ceiling. "I recall a large cache of drugs being recovered after the Corporation massacre."

Garrett nodded. Ella slurped her apple juice.

Sanjiv took a deep breath then stood. "There have also been some rumblings about the legitimacy of the Krotch's business interests. Speaking of rumblings, you must excuse me." She ran for the bathroom.

Ella turned to Garrett. "She sick?"

He nodded. "She has a baby in her tummy and sometimes

the mommy feels sick in the morning."

Fatima asked, "What do you think?"

"It's better than sitting back and taking crap from the Krotch boys. I just wonder if we can afford it. You just lost your business and ..." He held his hands open.

The door to the washroom opened. "Sorry about that. I was hoping this would be over with but-" Sanjiv held her hands in the air in the universal signal for "What can you do?" She sat down. "You were wondering about the cost?"

Garrett blushed, looking toward the bathroom.

Sanjiv said, "I'm a good listener. Anyway, my fee would be one third plus expenses. In other words, when we get a settlement from the Krotch brothers, I get one third plus my expenses."

Fatima said, "You think we'll win?"

"I think we have a good shot." She sipped her tea, looking at Ella. "Is it possible to get Sydney's contact information, please?"

Fatima asked, "Do you know something about the situation we don't?"

"I can tell you the brothers think they are smarter than everyone else, and their arrogance makes them vulnerable. To answer your question more directly, yes I do know something, but can not share it at this time."

TWENTY-SIX

Thursday, June 19

O

Sydney sat across the table from Gwen who asked, "Did she tell you why we had to meet on such short notice?" The sun shone through the picture window.

Gwen shook her head. "No." She wore a white blouse and slacks. "School will be over soon then Michael and Robert will be home." She looked around. "Where's Jackson?"

The linoleum felt cool on Sydney's feet. "Liam took him into Calgary. They're shopping for a new computer." She caught motion from the corner of her eye. Jean closed the back yard gate. "Here she is." Sydney walked to open the back door. "Mornin' Jean."

Jean smiled. She carried a massive rainbow striped bag over her left shoulder. She kicked off her running shoes, following Sydney into the kitchen.

Gwen asked, "How are you?"

Jean set her bag on a chair, pulling out a laptop. "I have something to show you. I think the Krotch brothers just made a big mistake." She opened the laptop, fiddling with the trackpad then typing her password. "They sent a copy of their latest email to Rodney's old email address."

Sydney asked, "Can I pour you a coffee?"

Jean nodded while turning the laptop so her friends could read. Sydney stood and Gwen sat as they leaned in.

Kristopher Krotch 19/06
To: Harold Krotch, Doug Brown, Steve Decker, Giles Patriot, Rodney Richardson
The following points will help clarify our plan to discredit Garrett MacGregor, derail the upcoming festival, and restore Corporation's former prominence as a hub for transport and manufacturing.

1. A series of articles in the *Upper Canada Press* will maintain the focus on MacGregor as an arsonist and opportunist. Giles, you are expected to spread the word about MacGregor's misdeeds on your radio show.
2. Doug, you will continue to gather intelligence on any and all individuals involved in the organization of the Canada Day festival. Exploit any opportunity to discredit these individuals and take the focus away from our operations.
3. Fergus MacGregor has agreed to offer more details about Garrett's background to further discredit him.
4. Preston and Robbie Decker have agreed to testify that Garrett paid them to set fire to his fiancé's business in order to collect the insurance. In exchange, the Deckers will recieve future considerations and legal representation.
5. Financial pressure will be put on MacGregor's son and daughter through our banking connections.
6. Bonuses of $200,000 each will be paid upon cancellation of the upcoming festival.

Kristopher Krotch
CEO Nova Bank
1(800) 525-3666

Headquaters: Toronto, ON, Canada
Founded: Toronto

Gwen looked over the screen and smiled at Jean. "Did you make hard copies?"

Jean reached into her bag, handing them each a paper copy. "I also emailed it to you."

Sydney went back to the counter, setting the coffee pot back in its cradle. She turned, leaning against the sink. "I think it's time."

Jean sat down, adding cream to her coffee.

Gwen glanced at the email.

Sydney said, "I got a call from Garrett's lawyer this morning. We need to send her a copy of the email." She pointed at the laptop. "Then we need to make an appointment with my superiors in Calgary and the video needs to be released. We have all we need now to go after the Krotch boys."

Gwen said, "It's hard to believe the Krotch boys are this stupid."

Sydney said, "And arrogant."

Jean said, "I'm tired of looking over my shoulder. Been doing that for too long. It's time for the Krotch boys to find out what it's like."

Gwen said, "They are vicious. The fire in Calgary is proof. We need to be careful."

. . . .

"Garrett?"

"Yes." He and Ella sat on the couch watching Shrek for the seventeenth time. She snuggled up against him while he held the phone.

"It's Sanjiv."

He sat up, stuffing his feet in sandals. "What's up?"

"There has been a significant development. Would you be able to come to my office tomorrow?"

"Good news?"

"I think so. Would three work?"

"Yes."

Sanjiv said, "See you then. Bye. Oh and if your children receive any unususal correspondence, bring it with you."

Fatima walked into the living room, putting her hand over her cell phone. "I've been on hold for ten minutes. Who was that?"

"Sanjiv wants to see me tomorrow. How's it going with insurance?"

Fatima shook her head. "Everything was fine until that *Upper Canada Press* article came out. The insurance company called and they're asking questions."

· · · · · · · · · · · · · · ·

"Dad?"

"David?" Garrett spoke into his cell phone as he walked alongside the Bow River. The water was more brown than green from spring runoff.

"Yep. I got this letter."

"You okay?" Garrett dodged a jogger with a stroller almost as wide as the paved trail.

"Better. This letter is from my bank. It says the Nova Bank wants to take over my mortgage."

Garrett looked out across the river. A pair of geese skimmed over a patch of white water. "Okay if I come over so I can take the letter to my lawyer?"

"Okay. Dad? Jac got one too."

TWENTY-SEVEN

Friday, June 20

O

Giles Patriot wore black headphones, checked the computer monitor on his right, then faced the one to his left. He adjusted his red golf shirt.

Billy was outside at the controls. "Ready to go?"

"I haven't had a dump in two days, and I've got a belly full of gas. I'm fuckin' ready to kick some ass!" Giles discharged a hippo fart. "Get that?"

"You're on in three."

Giles took a breath, exhaled. "Good morning and welcome to the Patriot Hour. Today we start with an editorial rant about con artists. The recent tragedies in Corporation have attracted the worst kind of self-serving, egotistical degenerates who arrive in the guise of saviours. In particular, I speak of one Garrett MacGregor who has been engaged by misguided local residents planning to hold a festival on Canada Day. It turns out Garrett MacGregor thinks he's above the law.

"The two men who set fire to the Calgary business of Fatima Delvechio are ready to testify they were paid to do the job by her fiancé who just happens to be Garrett MacGregor. To make matters worse, Garrett's brother has testified his brother risked his granddaughter's safety to portray himself as a hero.

"On Monday, more details will be revealed about Garrett MacGregor's fraudulent misrepresentations. He is the worst kind of con man. The kind who arrives after a tragedy to fill his pockets with the hard earned money of the grieving folks who call Corporation home.

"The people of Corporation must be protected from miscreants like Garrett MacGregor whose ego makes him believe he isn't required to live by the rules of civilized society."

• • • • • • • • • • • • • • •

Garrett sat across the table from Sanjiv. She wore a red blouse and oversized black palazzo pants borrowed from her brother's store. Sanjiv burped, took a deep breath, and let it out slow. Ella eyed the chocolates in the dish in the middle of the table. Fatima sat on the other side of the toddler, looking tired from riding the insurance industry carousel round and round from receptionist to agent, and back again.

He put a manila envelope on the table. "Both my kids got registered letters saying their banks intend to sign their mortgages over to Nova Bank. Fatima's insurance company has her stranded in some kind of beurocratic wasteland where double talk passes as conversation. I just want to know one thing."

Sanjiv sipped tea. "What's that?"

Fatima asked, "Will this get worse before it gets better?"

Sanjiv opened a file, sliding it across the table. "Please read this." Garrett and Fatima put their heads together to read the email from Kristopher Krotch.

Garrett lifted his eyes to see Sanjiv watching him over her teacup. "Where did you get this?"

Sanjiv shrugged. "A friend."

Fatima asked, "What do you plan to do with this?"

Sanjiv smiled. "I have some ideas I'd like to run past you."

Garrett said, "Okay."

"The first one is you will probably be approached by media outlets. My advice is to walk toward them and use short answers."

Fatima asked, "Like what?"

Sanjiv leaned forward. "If they ask you what you have to say try, 'The charges are false.' Or maybe, 'There is no truth to the allegations.' If they ask how you feel say, 'No one likes being lied about.' And if they say there are witnesses try, 'Look into the backgrounds of these witnesses.' In other words make the reporters do their due diligence. Journalists often say the guilty run from them and the innocent run to them. I say walk toward them."

Garrett shook his head. "What about the Krotch plan?"

Sanjiv nodded. "I will be firing back on Monday or Tuesday. I think the brothers will stick to their plan and more will be printed in their paper on the weekend. Let them dig a deeper hole, then we will have more dirt to throw on them and a bigger settlement."

Ella asked, "You talked to Sydney?"

Sanjiv smiled, looking from Garrett to Fatima then back to Ella. "I did, and they have plans to begin their own separate campaign on Monday. So I'm asking you to have a quiet weekend and follow the news next week. Can you do that?"

Garrett asked, "There is something else?"

Sanjiv took a breath. "The more dirt the Krotch boys throw on you, the more it will cost them in the end. That's the bottom line." She looked at Ella. "And things will probably get crazy in the immediate future." She looked at the door. "That's why I've hired some people to keep you safe."

Garrett's eyebrows went up. He held Ella closer. She said, "Bubby, you're sqeezing me!"

Fatima put her hand to her heart.

Sanjiv got up, opening the door of her office. Two women

in jeans, white blouses, and Harris-tweed sports coats eased through the door. They were just under six feet tall, weighing about two-twenty each, had short brown hair, and round faces. One had hazel eyes, the other blue. Sanjiv pointed at hazel eyes, "This is Hazel and her twin sister Indigo. They are assigned as your bodyguards."

Fatima pointed at herself, then at Garrett and Ella. "What about our kids?"

Indigo smiled, stepping forward, getting down on one knee, extending her hand to Ella. "I'm Indigo. What's your name?"

Ella lifted her chin. "Do you like chocolate?"

Indigo looked at Garrett. "How old is she?"

Garrett hugged Ella close. "Two."

Indigo looked at Fatima who nodded. "Wow! She is bright."

"Chocolate?" Ella pointed at the bowl at the centre of the table.

Indigo stood, reached for the bowl, took one chocolate, unwrapped it, popped it in her mouth, and smiled at Ella. "One of my weaknesses."

Ella held out her hand. "Chocolate?"

Indigo looked at Garrett who nodded. She took another chocolate, unwrapped it, handing it to Ella who said, "Thank you," before popping it in her mouth and closing her eyes.

Hazel made eye contact with Fatima. "We've already done a threat assessment with both of your families and would like to review it with you. Your ex-husband Marco and his presidency of the local Hells Angels chapter is a definite concern."

Fatima asked, "Presidency?"

Garrett asked, "What's the next step?"

Ella said, "More chocolate."

TWENTY-EIGHT

<u>Saturday, June 21</u>

0

<u>Upper Canada Press</u>
<u>Insurance Fraudster Faces Allegations of Abuse</u>

By Elizabeth Chevrolet

Further investigation of Garrett MacGregor and his fiancé Fatima Delvechio reveals some disturbing facts.

Ms. Delvechio's former husband is a Hells Angel president and long-standing member of the organization. He agreed to be interviewed by the Upper Canada Press.

Marco Delvechio confirmed he is president of the western chapter of The Hells Angels. He states, "Our organization is largely misunderstood by society. We are involved with various charities in the west."

When asked about MacGregor's character, Marco said, "He is a very disturbing individual. He used to be my daughter's teacher, since then he has become an influence in her life. There have been disturbing changes in her personality."

Marco was asked directly if he thought MacGregor had sexually assaulted his daughter. Delvechio said, "I have no evidence of that, but I do have my suspicions. As I said, my daughter has exhibited some disturbing personality changes, which I attribute to either physical or psychological abuse."

Mr. Delvechio also said he had no knowledge of the fire set at his ex-wife's business. Instead he said, "I've learned to be very suspicious of Garrett MacGregor's motives and question the treatment of his grand daughter. I personally witnessed Mr. MacGregor putting his granddaughter in a dangerous situation. I would never allow any member of my family to be placed in such danger."

When asked to be more specific about the danger MacGregor's grandchild found herself in, he declined further comment.

. . . .

"You sure you want to do this?" Fatima stuffed her feet into a pair of black pumps.

"I'm not going to hide. You don't have to come."

She looked at him with eyes that said, "Don't be stupid."

He shrugged, opening the front door. They made it as far as the sidewalk running parallel to the street in front of the condo when they heard, "Here they come!"

There was contempt in bodyguard Hazel's voice when she said, "Reporters."

Minivan doors slid open. Several microphones appeared. A still camera flashed. A shoulder held camera appeared.

A blonde woman asked, "Mr. MacGregor what do you have to say about reports you paid arsonists to burn down your fiancés business?"

Garrett faced the reporter, noticing perfect hair and makeup. "They are simply not true."

A male reporter in a grey suit stepped in front of Fatima. "Ms. Delvechio, your ex-husband says Mr. MacGregor is a negative influence on your daughter."

Fatima tucked her hair behind her ear. "Marco abandoned our daughter for ten years. How would he know one way or another?"

The man behind the camera asked, "Did you know he was president of the Hells Angels?"

Fatima shook her head. "I knew he had connections with the Angels, not that he was the president."

The reporter with the camera moved to his left to get a better angle. The edge of the curb caught him by surprise. He stumbled. Garrett reached out to stop him falling then asked, "You okay?"

The reporter said, "Thanks dude."

Garrett said, "We're going to Hexagon for a coffee. You can meet us there if you like." He took Fatima's hand, walking south with Hazel following behind.

Hazel spoke into her hand, "We're walking to Hexagon. You stay with the house."

Almost a block later, Fatima asked, "Why did you tell them where we're going?"

Garrett shrugged. "They would have followed us anyways, and we really have nothing to hide. We didn't set fire to your shop. We have no intention of harming Ella or Dayna."

"And?"

"I just think it'll all work out."

She squeezed his arm. "It's good you're back."

They reached a two-storey house with curved lines and yellow paint. "A Hobbit must live there."

Fatima laughed. "It's one of my customers. She gets her toes lasered because they're so hairy!"

They walked together to Kensington Road then east across 14th Street. Traffic was heavy.

They passed a couple of women going the other way. Both wore yoga pants and bright tops. As they passed, one woman said, "He's just so into his work." The other said, "Guys have no emotional intelligence."

Fatima put her hand on Garrett's shoulder and smiled. "I

was worried everyone was going to recognize us."

He shrugged.

Five minutes later they climbed the curved staircase to Hexagon. They opened the door, heard the hum of conversation, and inhaled the scent of coffee. Fatima led the way past the display case of desserts and cookies. The windows kept the interior bright. Ahead and behind, a blur of faces.

Fatima found a table while he ordered drinks. He looked up at the menu while waiting behind a man and woman who couldn't make up their minds.

Garrett did some mental beach travelling, deciding upon Port Dixon's Straights of Malacca white sand. Then he remembered walking down a gravel road on the way back from the beach. Macaque monkeys sat at the edge of the jungle. The large male licked his canines.

"What would you like?"

"Large London fog and large mocaccino to go, please." He handed over a twenty, and she handed back the change. He dropped a toonie in the tip jar, stashing the bills in his pocket, waiting by the bar for his order.

"Hi Mr. MacGregor."

Garrett turned to face a twenty something man who sat on the bench along the east wall. His hair was over his ears and collar, his beard about a week old, and his khaki shirt and jeans wrinkled. "Chris?"

Chris stuck out his hand. "Just home from U of Vic and came here to meet some friends. You still teaching?"

"Retired. You just about finished university?"

Chris lifted a paper coffee cup. "One more year."

The barista behind the red Rancilio espresso machine said, "Large London Fog and mocha on the bar!"

Garrett put lids on the cups then turned to Chris. "Good to see you."

Chris smiled. "You too."

Garrett walked over to Fatima who chose a table next to the window and overlooking Kensington Road. She was talking to a woman at the next table then turned, looking up as he set her cup down. "Thanks."

He pulled up a chair across from her. "See, no problem."

A pair of heels marched across the tiled floor. Heads lifted, turning, conversations ending. Elizabeth Chevrolet's blonde Dame Edna hair was Chinook proof. She wore a blue pinstriped jacket and pants. Black high-heeled boots reached her knees. Her grey eyes were focused on Garrett. Above them a pair of penciled in eyebrows. Below them, white foundation, rouge on the cheeks, and scarlet lipstick. She pointed a white fingernail at him. "Garrett MacGregor, *Upper Canada Press* has a few questions for you."

Chevrolet pulled a chair from a nearby table, sitting at the head of their table. Fatima said, "Join us, why don't you?"

Garrett got a whiff of whiskey and second hand menthol. He coughed to clear his throat. "How are you?" *Just remember, she hates being called Chevy.*

Elizabeth reached into her red bag.

Fatima asked, "Got another bottle in there?"

Chevrolet pulled out a tape recorder, setting it on the table.

Garrett took a breath, looking across the table at Fatima who shook her head with an expression that said, "You wouldn't listen to me so don't tell me what I can and can't say."

Chevrolet turned to Garrett. "What do you have to say about Marco Delvechio's accusation of physical and psychological abuse of his daughter?"

Fatima's face went magenta. "You take the word of a deadbeat Hells Angels dad who never paid one dollar in child support and who recently disowned his daughter? How is Marco a reliable source of anything but bullshit?"

Chevrolet ignored Fatima, pointing at Garrett. "Are you avoiding answering the question?"

You know it's only this quiet in here at seven am. He looked at Chevrolet's fluorescent smile and was reminded of the Malay macaque at the edge of the jungle eyeing him like he was under glass at a casino buffet.

"Why don't you answer Fatima's question, Chevy?" The woman at the next table got up, standing to one side of Chevrolet. The woman had short black hair, a pronounced nose and jaw. Her irises switched from brown to black.

Chevrolet said, "I'm conducting this interview. Kindly let us finish."

"No. This isn't an interview. It's trial by media. If your past articles are any indication, you're not interested in facts." The woman crossed her arms under her breast.

Garrett thought, *This must be the woman Fatima talked about. She had breast cancer and decided against reconstructive surgery. I think her name's Janice.*

"So this is a set up?" Chevrolet pointed at Garrett. "You got your friends here ahead of time."

Garrett shook his head.

Janice waved a finger in front of Chevrolet's nose. "Nobody tells me what to say or do. And I still want an answer to Fatima's question. Why are you listening to Marco the deadbeat dad?"

Chevrolet turned to Garrett. "You brother says you staged the disappearance of your granddaughter so you could look like a hero."

Garrett said, "You work for the Krotch boys. So does my brother. Do you believe in coincidences?"

Chevrolet pointed a finger at her chest. "No one questions my integrity!"

Fatima started the laughter. Janice joined in, helping it to spread.

Garrett saw the mean girl, high school rage in Chevrolet's glare. He shrugged. She stood. The chair smacked the floor with its back. Chevrolet turned, walking out. Someone tapped him on the shoulder. It was Chris with a phone in his hand. "You didn't think we believed that crap she wrote about you?"

TWENTY-NINE

Sunday, June 22

O

"Garrett MacGregor, this is Darr, you know, your lawyer's brother?"

How did you get this number? Garrett strolled across the playing field on the east side of Queen Mary School on his way to an early afternoon walk along the Bow River. Indigo walked at his side. *Where did all the reporters go?*

"I pestered my sister until she gave me your number. I hope you don't mind."

Garrett stopped, looking at the medieval architecture of what was now Queen Mary's drama department. "What's up?"

"Some of us queens got together last night for a performance. One is a welder from Corporation. Anyway, we got to talking and the Calgary queens would like to join the Canada Day festivities if we could."

Garrett closed his eyes, turning to feel the sun on his face. "We'd be glad to have you there. You just need to confirm with Riley and Sam." He gave Darr the number.

"Thanks."

"How's Sanjiv feeling?"

"You're a darling to ask. Talked to her this morning. She's got her feet up."

"Say hello to Riley and Sam for me."

"Will do." Darr ended the call.

Garrett put the phone in his pocket, turning to Indigo. "Any idea where the reporters went?"

• • • • • • • • • • • • • • •

Gwen looked across her kitchen table at Jean and Sydney. "We're ready to go then?"

Jean took a breath before nodding.

Sydney asked, "Can I read those articles one last time please?"

Gwen opened her laptop, lifting the screen, typing the password, and swinging it around for Sydney to read. As always, her face was a closed book.

THIRTY

Monday, June 23

0

Upper Canada Press

Abusive Octogenarian Threatens Reporter

By Elizabeth Chevrolet

Sometimes, not very often, but sometimes, my nose fails me. I should have smelled a rat when Garrett MacGergor said he was going to his neighbourhood coffee shop.

I went into the coffee shop alone to ask Mr. MacGregor and his fiancée Fatima Delvechio some questions. Among the questions was MacGregor's alleged physical and psychological abuse of Dayna Delvechio and the staged disappearance of his granddaughter.

He refused to answer either question. Instead he avoided answers and let his fiancée speak for him. Then another woman (my instincts say she was a plant) began to attack the integrity of this reporter.

I've known many men like Garrett MacGregor in my time. They attack the integrity of others, because they have none of their own.

In time, the true character of this man will be exposed, this reporter and the UCP are determined it will happen.

. . . .

"I am Giles Patriot and this is the Patriot Hour. The Machiavellian nature of Garrett MacGregor has been revealed. *Upper Canada Press* columnist Elizabeth Chevrolet describes how MacGregor and his fiancée ambushed her.

"Ms. Chevrolet arrived at a Calgary coffee shop to ask MacGregor some hard questions about his recent malfeasance. It was a set up. A hostile crowd of misinformed supporters of arsonist MacGregor and his Hells Angels fiancée accosted the famed UCP reporter.

"Thankfully, Elizabeth was uninjured and had the courage to write about the experience.

"Citizens of Corporation would be well advised to steer clear of MacGregor. Shakespeare wrote truth will out. And he was right. The truth about Garrett MacGregor is coming out. He is no friend of the people of Corporation. His manipulation of the emotions of grieving citizens is unconscionable. He is a man with not one single shred of integrity."

. . . .

YYC News
Leaked Video Paints New Picture

A video of a confrontation between Elizabeth Chevrolet and Garrett MacGregor has gone viral.

Two years ago MacGregor became a social media phenom. A video of him being hit over the head by a bottle swinging Chevrolet went viral. Chevrolet became famous for saying, "I struck a blow for all women."

The more recent confrontation occurred at a Calgary coffee shop called Hexagon on Saturday. It shows Chevrolet attempting to ask MacGregor and fiancée Fatima Delvechio some questions. It appears Chevrolet's account of the event in the

Monday morning Upper Canada Press left out some significant details. There is considerable *buzz on social media reacting to her perceived inaccuracies.*

. . . .

YYC News

Krotch Family in Hot Water

By Gwen Chorny
This will be the first of five installments detailing the operations of brothers Kristopher and Harold Krotch. The pair is often touted in the Upper Canada Press (a newspaper owned by the Krotch brothers) as the richest men in Canada.

The Krotch brothers inherited their fortune from their late father Kevin Karl Krotch who built an oil and gas empire before branching into communications. The late Krotch senior was tried and convicted of sexual assault and sexual interference with three girls under fourteen. He was sentenced to fifteen years in prison.

Kristopher and Harold were concerned for their father's safety and hired three brothers to protect their father while in prison in Alberta's Bowden Institution.

A long time guard at the prison told me that, "It was common knowledge that triplets Robbert, Preston, and Steven Decker were Kevin Krotch's bodyguards. Anyone who interfered with Kevin Karl Krotch would have to answer to the triplets."

The Decker triplets were convicted of possession of a controlled substance for the purpose of trafficking. Documents confirm their incarceration at the Bowden Institution coincided with that of the senior Krotch.

Robert and Preston Decker were recently in the news and are charged with arson. Their lawyer – and Upper Canada Press – maintain the Decker brothers were hired by Garrett MacGregor. A recent email from Kristopher Krotch dated June ninth outlined a "plan to discredit Garrett MacGregor, de-

rail the upcoming festival, and restore Corporation as a hub for transport and manufacturing."

This is concrete evidence indicating the Krotch brothers are fabricating accusations aimed at Mr. MacGregor.

Tomorrow's installment will explain the connection between the Nova Bank —of which the Krotch brothers are co chairs and majority shareholders—and K&K Real Estate of Calgary.

. . . .

"Garrett?"

"Hey Sanjiv. How are you feeling?" Garrett sat next to Fatima on the couch. They were watching a movie on her big screen.

"Fatima should hear from her insurance company today." Garrett leaned forward. "Everything okay?"

"I think so. Have you been following the YYC and *Upper Canada Press?*"

"No."

"Maybe you should. Call me right after you hear from Fatima's insurance company. Talk with you soon." She hung up.

. . . .

"Dad?"

He heard the emotion in Jac's voice. "What's happened?"

"David didn't come home from work. He's not answering his phone."

. . . .

Indigo rode shotgun. She took up more than half of the cabin while Garrett drove west along Crowchild Trail. "You should let me drive."

Garrett had his four way flashers on, flicking his high beams at a black Escalade in the far left lane. The Escalade was doing the speed limit, effectively blocking three lanes while two other drivers matched the black SUV's speed. "Get over asshole!"

Indigo put a hand on Garrett's shoulder. "Take a breath, then take another, or pull over, and let me drive."

Garrett glanced at her nails. They were blue with gold glitter. He took a breath, then another, and backed off from the Escalade.

Indigo said, "Now we go to David's school and work our way back to some of his familiar haunts."

Ten minutes later, Garrett pulled into the parking lot at David's school. It was just north of the river in amongst two storey homes and three car garages sprinkled along a bluff of acreages. A woman walked toward a white Buick. Garrett pulled up behind. His window hummed. "Hello."

The woman was over six feet, had grey short cut hair, and a smile. "You're David's dad."

Garrett recognized David's principal but couldn't remember her name. "Do you have any idea where he went after school?"

The principal put her hand on the roof of Garrett's Ford, leaning over. She looked at Indigo and her black blazer. "What's happened?"

"I don't know what David's told you, but his phone is off, and he hasn't come home." Garrett tried to keep his voice matter-of-fact and succeeded, sort of.

"I know a little bit." She hesitated. "He said something about going to see a movie to get his mind off things."

"Thank you." Garrett waited for her to lean away from the car, drove out of the lot, then east into the city. They parked near the Cineplex.

Indigo said, "There's an open spot."

They climbed out, heading for the front doors. Inside, Garrett looked at the posters on the walls. He spotted one that looked likely with buff men, guns, and leggy women with perfect hair. "That one." He inhaled the scents of popcorn and oil, spilled pop, French fries, and sugar.

Indigo said, "Keep going."

Garrett saw the ticket taker was busy with a line up, so he looked away, walking right, and heading for theatre two. He stepped past the garbage can, opening the door. He was cocooned in blue light. His right hand touched the wall and he walked to the corner, waiting for his eyes to adjust. Silhouettes of shoulders and heads became more distinct. Indigo tapped him on the left shoulder. The big screen went from night to dawn. Garrett looked to his left. David's face was lit up. His head shaved close, his red beard cut short, and his grey eyes focused on the screen. Garrett sat down next to his son who looked right, then looked back at the screen where a man held the wrist of a woman dangling over a precipice.

A man two rows in front said, "Turn your damned phone off!"

A narrow faced woman with a pixie cut sat two rows in front of the man. The face of her phone was bright blue. She held it up. "No!"

The man leaned forward. "We're trying to watch the movie."

Pixie cut spoke into her phone, "Oh it's some jerk sitting behind me."

The male hero on the screen dragged the woman back from the precipice.

Someone to the left said. "Shut your god damned phone off!"

Pixie stood up, pointing her phone at her chest. "I've got a PhD!"

The man said, "So?"

Pixie said, "I'm going to pray to God for you!"

Someone near David said, "What's God got to do with it!"

Indigo touched Garrett's shoulder. "We need to go."

A shower of ice from a soft drink cup flashed in front of the movie stars, slapping the side of Pixie's head.

Indigo pulled Garrett to his feet, shoving him toward the door, grabbing David, then following. More people stood. Popcorn, punches, and ice flew. The theatre erupted into a brawl.

Garrett, David, and Indigo walked out into the carpeted hallway. The door shut behind them. They walked toward the entrance where people chatted, bought popcorn and drinks, and stood in line. "Keep moving," Indigo said. She held her left hand open as they stepped outside into the summer heat.

David turned to his father. "Shit's never dull when you're around dad."

Indigo touched Garrett's arm. "Okay if you and your son ride together, and I follow in your car?" Garrett reached into his pocket, tossing the keys to Indigo.

David began to talk after they turned onto Stoney Trail, pushing the rental up over ninety kilometers an hour. The sunroof was open, the wind buffeted them, and they talked loud to compensate. "Mom called me from Toronto."

Garrett waited. *Fuck!* "Okay."

"She invited me to come and visit her and Fergus."

You were always the one who was closest to Marie when you were little. "That's nice."

"I asked her why Fergus lied about Ella getting lost in the mall."

Garrett closed his eyes, feeling the wind waving across two of the three hairs on the top of his head.

"She said I could learn a lot from Fergus' pragmatism, and how it made him so successful with his career."

Garrett opened his eyes, staring at the belly of an overpass.

The sound of their engine echoed back at them.

"I asked her if pragmatism was the same as betrayal. She told me I should have more respect for her and Fergus."

Blame the victim. Never take responsibility. Do your damage, then move on to bigger and better things. Marie and Fergus are perfect for one another.

"Dad–" David kept his eyes on the road. "–why did I fall in love with a woman who's just as self-centred as my mother?"

Garrett shrugged. "The thing is now you see it. I think that's how we come to gather knowledge. It may be beautiful or it may be ugly, but it's all knowledge. And inevitably that ability to see people for who they are protects us."

David glanced right. "That was profound!"

"You liked it?" Garrett grinned.

"Almost as much as that lady with the PhD!"

Garrett laughed.

David asked, "What' new on the wedding plans?"

Laughter stopped.

"Dad, Fatima is a keeper. Get on it!"

205

THIRTY-ONE

Tuesday, June 24

0

I am Giles Patriot and this is the Patriot Hour. The story of
the deviant Garrett MacGregor gets murkier as news of his
latest exploits reach our ears.

"MacGregor's lawyer Sanjiv Sandhu–more on her later–
revealed she will represent MacGregor in his lawsuit against
the illustrious Canadian entrepreneurs Kristopher and Harold
Krotch. These two Canadian pillars of society, media moguls,
honorary members of the Patriot Institute, Order of Canada
recipients, and philanthropists are the latest targets of a
desperate and malevolent man.

"Sandhu charges the Krotch brothers with systematically
and maliciously setting out to ruin the reputation of her client.
We all know Mr. MacGregor's reputation as an opportunist
and child abuser. His lawyer Ms. Sandhu plays the role of
upstanding solicitor, while she operates an office next door
to her brother Darr Sanhu. He operates a store in Calgary
frequented by men who acquire the attire of women. Sanjiv
and Darr Sandhu are attempting to sully the reputations of two
of Canada's patriots. And I say Canadians will not stand for
this!

"Kristopher and Harold Krotch have personally assured

me they will fight any and all attempts to smear their reputations."

. . . .

YYC News

Krotch Brothers Flex Deep Pockets

by Gwen Chorny

Access to communications between the Krotch brothers and former Corporation mayor Rodney Richardson reveals unsettling facts. In order to understand these revelations, some background is required.

Kristopher and Harold Krotch are majority shareholders and sit on the board of Nova Bank. Nova is the second largest bank in Canada.

Nova Bank wholly owns K&K Realty based in Calgary. K&K brokers real estate deals, and Nova provides the mortgages.

One more important fact needs to be understood. In the drug trade, money and drugs almost never come together. Payment for the manufacturing, distribution, and sale of drugs is often accomplished through real estate transactions. Again, communications be-

tween the Krotch brothers, K&K Realty, Nova Bank, and Rodney Richardson reveal how real estate purchases were handled on Richardson's five properties.

The Richardson lakeside property in Corporation is valued at 2.5 million. Richardson paid no money down, then paid one hundred dollars a month to Nova Bank for his mortgage.

The Richardson estate owns a twenty-unit condo property in Calgary. Richardson collected rent on each unit. Again Nova Bank purchased the property through K&K realty. All contractors were paid by Nova. The mayor of Corporation contributed a grand total of one thousand dollars to construction costs, and his estate owns the property outright.

The Richardson estate also owns a thirteen-storey condo apartment complex on the western edge of downtown

Calgary. Again, Richardson contributed one thousand dollars in construction costs, and his estate owns the property.

The Richardson estate owns a 3.5 million mansion on Lake Windermere in BC. The ten-year amortized mortgage monthly payment is one hundred and fifty dollars.

Finally, there is a 10.3 million property in La Jolla, California owned outright by the Richardson estate.

Rodney Richardson's yearly salary as mayor of Corporation was fifty-five thousand dollars. He inherited three sections of land when his father died. The land is valued at 1.5 million dollars.

Tomorrow's article will outline the Krotch brothers' plan to discredit Garrett MacGregor and sabotage Corporation's upcoming Sausage Festival on Canada Day.

• • • • • • • • • • • • •

Garrett pushed Ella in the stroller as they made their way along Kensington Road. Neither Indigo nor Hazel followed. Instead it was a mountain named Thomas. He was six six, wore black shorts, and a black dress shirt with a tie. His beard was lumberjackesque, his hands were bigger than pie plates, and his shoes at least size fourteen. Ella had taken a shine to him right away. She asked, "Tommy?"

Thomas moved up alongside, leaning down when Garrett stopped. Ella asked, "You like coffee?"

"Yes, I think I'll join Garrett in a mocaccino." He stood up, and they continued east to the lights at Fourteenth Street.

Garrett's phone rang. He fished it out of his shirt pocket, recognized the number, and answered. "What's up Riley?"

"Just checking on how you're doing. Patriot is doing his rants, and as far I can tell most people are laughing at him. Gwen's articles are making Doug Brown and Steve Decker nervous. I'm sorry you and Fatima are taking so much of the flak."

Garrett shrugged as the walk sign turned white, Thomas looked all around, and they crossed Fourteenth Street. "My lawyer is handling it all. There's a bodyguard right here with Ella and me."

"You've got a bodyguard?"

"His name is Thomas. He has partners named Indigo and Hazel."

"Sorry." Riley inhaled. "I don't know how I'm gonna make this up to you."

"Any news on the wedding plans?" Garrett lifted the front wheel of the stroller up onto the sidewalk.

"Sam's got it all figured. The church and minister are booked. He's taken care of the food. It all happens the day of the festival. The only things you need to worry about are getting yourself there, the rings, and the license. One of Jean's friends is making the cake."

"Rings?" Garrett felt sweat rolling down his ribs.

"You forgot about the rings? It's a week from today!"

Thomas said, "I bet Diva Darr can help with the rings."

Ella looked over her shoulder. "Go see Darr?"

211

THIRTY-TWO

Wednesday, June 25

0

YYC News
Corporation Bigwigs on Krotch Payroll

by Gwen Chorny

One of the more insidious aspects of the Krotch Empire is their penchant for discrediting those they identify as threats.

In a leaked email, Kristopher Krotch outlined his plan to discredit Corporation's upcoming Canada Day celebrations, otherwise known as Corporation's First Annual Sausage Festival.

The primary target of the Krotch smear is Garrett Mac-Gregor. Mr. Krotch's motive is to "restore Corporation as a hub for transport and manufactur-

ing." This is a direct reference to the Nova Bank and K&K Realty drug manufacturing, distribution, and money laundering enterprises overseen by former Mayor Rodney Richardson. It is important to note this email is addressed to Doug Brown and Giles Patriot who are promised "Bonuses of $200,000 will be paid upon cancellation of the upcoming festival."

A copy of the email in its entirety follows this article. The original has been forwarded to the RCMP.

Jean sat on her back porch, drinking iced tea in the shade. She looked at the pitcher sweating a ring onto the glass tabletop. Then she kicked off her sandals, putting her feet up on the seat of the next chair, inspecting the fresh purple coat on her toenails. She leaned her head back, stretching her arms out, checking the camera. It was attached to the limb of her crabapple tree. Nearby, the microphone hung down from a separate limb. She leaned forward, checking the second camera pointed ninety degrees away from the first, nestled between marigolds in the flower box. Luke was in her basement sipping coffee, monitoring the cameras on his laptop.

She was pouring a second glass of iced tea when the back gate opened. Jean felt her muscles tense. The pitcher chimed when glass met glass. She took a deep breath to settle her nerves.

"Good morning." Doug Brown with his immaculately combed blonde hair and moustache walked ahead of Giles Patriot. Patriot walked with control. One foot in front of the other, concentrating on maintaining a boozy balance.

Jean noted Patriot was already inebriated, realizing it made him more vulnerable, and more dangerous. "What can I do for you fellows?"

Brown pulled out a lawn chair, sitting across the table from her. Patriot crossed his arms, leaning against the house, cutting off her other avenue of escape.

Brown said, "You've been sharing emails with Gwen Chorny."

Jean sipped her iced tea to collect her thoughts. *Luke has called Sydney by now.* "Your point is?"

Patriot said, "We're not stupid. We know what you've been up to! The email had to have come from you because you had access!"

Brown looked at Patriot, pushing his open hand toward the ground, indicating Patriot should drop the volume.

Jean took her feet off the chair, tucking them into her sandals. She could smell the alcohol and Patriot's mint flavoured mouthwash. "So your bosses sent you here to shut me up?"

Brown leaned back in his chair, smiling. "That would be nice. A retraction stating you wrote the email would be even nicer."

Jean leaned forward. "Or?"

Patriot leaned forward, stumbling, managing to regain his balance by grabbing onto a chair. "You live alone. We can get to you."

Jean covered her mouth at the stink of second hand alcohol and sweat radiating from Patriot, realizing it was the stink of fear. "The Krotch brothers must be pretty worried sending you two over here like this."

Patriot said, "They're powerful men who like to protect their interests."

Brown shook his head, holding up his hands to stop Patriot.

Patriot either ignored him or didn't see the warning. "Kris and Harry have a lot of friends." He looked at Brown. "They can afford to hire him and me." Patriot pointed at his chest then at Brown. He faced Jean and said, "And they can afford to fucking destroy you."

Jean said, "Like they destroyed Cathy and Melvin's boy Derek?"

Brown nodded. "I hear you. That was very unfortunate, but they can't be held accountable for that. Nobody forced Derek to take meth."

Jean stood, concentrating on keeping her voice clear. "So you're saying that you two, Richardson, Milo, and the Krotch boys aren't responsible, and that Derek and Melvin are collateral damage?"

Patriot pointed at his chest. "We're the victims here."

Jean laughed. She pointed at each of them. "You're the victims?" Her eyes narrowed. She focused on Patriot. "What about the video? Are you and the Krotch boys victims in the video?"

Brown stood. He looked at Giles. "What video?"

The back gate opened. The pair turned at the rasp of hinges.

Sydney wore her RCMP uniform. She walked along the sidewalk, then onto the grass. "Good morning."

Jean saw the muscles tense on either side of Brown's spine. He asked, "Come to join us for some iced tea?"

Patriot's voice quivered. "Why'd you shoot Rod in the eye? You didn't have to shoot him in the eye."

Sydney put her right hand on the butt of her Glock, watching Patriot.

The back door opened. Constable Larry Sutherland ducked through to stand on the deck behind Jean. Larry nodded at Sydney who turned to Jean and said, "We got a phone call saying there was a disturbance at this address." She looked at Giles then at Brown. "You fellas mind explaining what you're doing here?"

Doug smiled, holding his hands down and away from his rodeo belt buckle. "Just having a friendly chat."

Patriot lifted his head. "I was asking Jean if she'd be on my show."

Jean said, "Bullshit."

Brown grinned. "Apparently, we have a difference of opinion."

Sydney turned to Jean. "Would you like a restraining order against these individuals? If so, you'll need to come to the detachment and fill out a statement of claim."

"Just a God damned minute!" Patriot raised a finger in the

air. Sydney faced him. The finger dropped.

Jean said, "Gladly. Let me get my purse. I would also like them to leave now."

Sydney lifted her right hand, pointing at the back gate. "Gentlemen."

She followed Patriot and Brown as they turned, walked, opened the gate, and stepped into the alley.

Larry said, "Give us a call if they bother you again."

"Thank you." Jean watched Larry walk to the back gate. Luke opened the screen door. She asked, "Did you get it?"

Luke nodded as he studied her with his brown eyes. He stepped outside, wrapping an arm around her shoulders. "You okay?"

"It's funny, but I feel great. Standing up to those two was just what I needed." She looked up at him. "They are so predictable."

Luke gave her a squeeze then released her. "I'm gonna get busy on the video. Things are moving pretty fast, and I want to be ready."

. . . .

Ella worked on the grapes Garrett had cut in half and put in a plastic cup. She sat on his lap and across the table from a man who wore a pair of jeweler's magnifying eyeglasses. Ella had been a bit taken aback until Rowan allowed her to look through the glasses then she went back to eating her grapes.

Rowan's shop was a block east and south of Diva Darr's, on the main floor of a two storey house built in the nineteen twenties. The oak floors creaked and groaned. The main room was lit by natural light from refurbished wood-framed windows. The walls were a light grey, adorned with stylized acrylic paintings of buildings in Inglewood. They were somewhere in between Dali's surrealism and Kurelek's vivid prairie hues.

Rowan opened a book to show them a variety of ring styles. "I have some of these in stock. Let's start here, because we have a time limit." He stroked his black beard. It began at the tips of his ears, reaching the centre of his chest. His head shone under the overhead lights.

Garrett pointed at a white gold ring with a single diamond. He leaned close to read the description. *It's called a Bainsville.*

Ella shook her head, pointing at another white gold band with multiple diamonds set inside what looked like a wheel. Garrett leaned closer, seeing it was a Baguette eternity ring. He looked at Rowan. "It has multiple diamonds?"

"Yes, and I have one in stock."

Ella looked at Garrett. She held a half grape in the air. "Good. Buy it." She popped the grape in her mouth.

"What's her size?" Rowan pulled open a drawer, revealing a clear plastic box. He set the box atop the table. He picked out one white gold ring, sliding the black ring sizing mandrel inside.

Ella said, "Nine."

Garrett looked at her. *How the hell did you know that?*

She picked up another grape, looking at him. "Dayna told me."

Twenty minutes later, she sat on his shoulders as they walked toward Deva Darr's. Garrett crouched and Ella ducked her head when they stepped through the door to Sanjiv's office. They sat down on the couch across from Kelly's desk. He was on the phone and waved while Garrett lifted Ella over his head to set her on the couch. She leaned her head against his arm. He lifted it, hugging her close. He looked at the pictures on the wall. It was an eclectic mixture of colour and black and white. One was an elaborate Toller Cranston print of a married couple on a white horse. Next to it was a black and white photo of two preteen girls in tutus and tights posing in the fifth position. The one on the right was Sanjiv and the other was.... Garrett glanced at Kelly who wore a white shirt and black tie. He watched Garrett then said to the person on the other end of the phone, "See you then." Kelly hung up the phone, resting his chin on his knuckles.

Garrett nodded at the picture. "That's a beautiful shot of you and Sanjiv."

Kelly smiled. "We've been friends since elementary school."

The door to the office swung open. A man in a grey three-piece suit carried a flower box under his arm. His hair was styled and grey in all the right places. His fingers were manicured. His black shoes gleamed. He pointed the flower box at Kelly. "I must see Ms. Sandhu right away."

Kelly said, "She's with a client at the moment Mr. Roberts."

The door to Sanjiv's office opened. Fatima stepped though followed by Sanjiv who said, "The cheque is supposed to arrive by tomorrow. We'll call when the courier drops it off."

Fatima spotted Garrett and Ella, sitting down next to them.

Mr. Roberts set the flower box on Kelly's desk, opening it. "Ms. Sandhu I need to speak with you urgently." He pulled out a wand. It was at least two feet long and made of clear plastic. The handle had an ornate guard roughly the shape of a figure eight. Above that was a curved shaft and circumcised tip. He flipped a switch on the handle. A series of colours–beginning with purple and finishing with orange–ran up the shaft. "It's a disaster! I ordered two thousand for the sausage festival!"

Sanjiv took a breath. Kelly had his hand over his mouth. Fatima bit her bottom lip. Garrett shrugged. Ella smiled.

Sanjiv asked, "What's a disaster?"

Roberts wove the wand above his head. "I tried it out at home and Regina had a seizure!"

Sanjiv took one step closer. "Who's Regina?"

Roberts lifted his chin. "My cat!"

Kelly coughed, reaching for his coffee cup.

The wand flashed. The rainbow walked its way up the shaft. Roberts waved it back and forth. The colours blurred. "What can I do? It's too late to return them all. I've spent a lot of money on these."

Sanjiv leaned a hip against Kelly's desk. "There probably won't be any cats at the festival."

"But what if-" He pointed the wand at her. "-it causes seizures in people?"

Sanjiv opened her hand, looking around the room, then back at Roberts.

Ella said, "He's weird."

To his credit, even Mr. Roberts joined the laughter. Ella hid her face against Garrett's ribs, embarrassed by the uproar she'd created.

THIRTY-THREE

Thursday, June 26

0

YYC News

Town Rises Up Against Injustice

by Gwen Chorny

Corporation, Alberta is a town on the edge of the foothills. It's close to major highways. It boasts a thriving Main Street and a majority of residents who enjoy quiet privacy. Unfortunately, this makes it an ideal location for drug manufacturing, transportation, and distribution.

When Kristopher and Harold Krotch purchased ten acres near the Corporation Lake, ostensibly to build a pair of ten million dollar mansions, it provided jobs and opportunities for townsfolk. That was

fifteen years ago. Gradually, the town realized the economic opportunity came at a price.

Rodney Richardson ran for mayor. Despite persistent rumours of his connections to the drug trade, and because two other candidates were encouraged to drop out, Richardson was acclaimed. Upper Canada Press, as well as the local radio station's celebrity, Giles Patriot, supported him. Remember, both news outlets are wholly owned by Nova Bank. The Krotch brothers own Nova.

Gradually, quietly, a drug manufacturing, transportation

and distribution network was built. Corporation became its hub. One of its victims was Derek Gartner who became addicted to methamphetamines. His father was Melvin Gartner, Corporation's barber. He was one of the men killed this spring on Richardson's property. An RCMP investigation of the massacre discovered a drug-manufacturing lab on the site.

The fallout resulted in a public relations nightmare for the Krotch brothers. They used the UCP and Giles Patriot to muddy the waters and shift the *blame. Then they used their connections to the Hells Angels to hire three brothers who had protected their father in prison.*

The Krotch brothers didn't anticipate two problems: the town of Corporation wants nothing more to do with them. And there is also disturbing video shot by one of Richardson's partners. Either he wanted the video for insurance in case the Krotch brothers decided to replace him, or it was intended for blackmail.

The video is the subject of tomorrow's article.

. . . .

"I am Giles Patriot and this is the Patriot Hour. Today's program will be abbreviated. I have an appointment to meet and an announcement to make.

"Some of you may know I have been fighting a battle with the demon known as alcohol for many years. For the last year, I have endeavoured to stay sober on the weekends with the intention of gradually adding one day every month. My plan has failed.

"After many valiant attempts at beating my addiction, I have come to the conclusion that rehabilitation is my next step.

"The recent passing of my good friend Rodney Richardson brought the crisis to a head. Rod was a great supporter and patriot like my good friends Kristopher and Harold Krotch. With the support of my friends, both deceased and living, I sign off for the present, and look toward an undiscovered future without alcohol."

• • • • • • • • • • • • • •

Upper Canada Press
<u>Lying Freelancer Sued by Krotch Family</u>

By Elizabeth Chevrolet

Kristopher and Harold Krotch intend to sue Gwen Chorny for fifty million dollars.

Recent articles by free-lancer Gwen Chorny are defamatory and libelous according to Kristopher Krotch.

When asked about the Chorny articles, Kristopher said, "The tragic deaths of the individuals massacred at Rodney Richardson's property have affected both my brother and me deeply. The heartless exploitation of this tragedy by Chorny is unconscionable. We continue to be touched and bolstered by the outpouring of support from right thinking Canadians."

Kristopher continued, "Both Harold and I have been reeling from the recent loss of our father who was recognized with an Order of Canada. The loss of our friend Rodney Richardson compounded our sense of loss. To have the reputations of both of these great Canadians impugned when they are no longer alive to defend themselves is an act of cowardice, which cannot remain unchallenged. We vow to fight these spurious allegations."

• • • • • • • • • • • • • •

Fatima grabbed her car keys. "That was Sanjiv. I have to go and pick up the cheque from the insurance company." She looked at Ella. "You coming?"

Ella stuffed a strawberry in her mouth, lifting her arms. Garrett grabbed a wipe, getting to work on Ella's face while she swung her head from side to side. He said, "Hold still then we can go to see Sanjiv and Darr."

Ella looked up at him and glared. Her face turned red.

Fatima said, "Oh shit! I'll get a new diaper."

It took about ten minutes to change the diaper, wipe Ella's backside, change her clothes, and take out the garbage. When all was done, Garrett sat Ella on his knee. "Would you please tell me when you need to go to the bathroom?"

Ella looked back at him. "I wipe my face myself?"

Garrett nodded. "Deal. Do we shake hands?"

Ella frowned. "Wash your hands first."

Fatima said, "I think you both need to wash your hands." She aimed Ella in the direction of the bathroom. Garrett followed her in, lifting her up on the step in front of the sink.

Ten minutes later, they were in Garrett's car heading along Memorial Drive. The Bow River was green and glistening in the morning sun. Cyclists weaved around dog walkers and joggers. Ella watched them, pointing a finger against the glass. "Boat!"

The fire department's aluminum jet boat growled upstream.

Traffic was light after rush hour. They made it to Diva Darr's in fifteen minutes. Garrett parked out front next to two news vans. Fatima said, "Karah alaikum!"

Ella said, "Smile!"

Fatima asked, "Should we come back later?"

Garrett opened his door. "Sanjiv said it's better to go toward the media." He shut his door, feeling anxiety running laps around his large intestine. He opened Ella's door, releasing her harness. He picked her up, and she planted herself on his hip.

Fatima shrugged, opening the door. Deva Darr smiled, cocking his head to the left. "You're just in time for the party." He followed them into Sanjiv's office.

Inside they saw Sanjiv in a white blouse and blue skirt.

Kelly stood beside her. Two reporters stood in front of them. Cameras flanked them. The white-haired male reporter with the microphone asked, "What is your reaction to the Krotch brothers plan to file a counter suit against your client?"

Garrett's lower intestine contracted and he winced.

Sanjiv put her hand to her mouth, swallowing. "Excuse me. The timing of the counter suit is suspicious. In my view, news of a video being released tomorrow has prompted this suit. It is an obvious attempt to intimidate my clients."

The blonde female reporter asked, "What is your opinion of the Krotch activities in Corporation, Alberta?"

Sanjiv smiled. "Which activities in particular?"

The blonde said, "Money laundering."

Sanjiv took a sip of tea. "I've been following the Chorny articles with interest. It appears the Krotch Empire has some difficult questions to answer. They have a long history of deflecting the media's attention when their business practices are called into question."

Kelly said, "Even Elizabeth Chevrolet has cut ties with *Upper Canada Press* and the Krotch boys. She announced her resignation this morning."

The male reporter asked, "When was this announced?"

Kelly pointed at her computer screen and an article under a red banner. "*Upper Canada Press* columnist Elizabeth Chevrolet announces resignation."

Garrett cleared his throat. "Maybe you should be asking why Chevrolet resigned?"

The cameras turned on him. Ella shaded her eyes with her right hand. The blonde stuck her microphone under Garrett's chin. "You think Chevrolet's resignation has something to do with tomorrow's video?"

Garrett shrugged. "I can't speak for Chevrolet. It seems more than a coincidence if both Patriot and Chevrolet step away from this controversy. I would ask why they are running away from the story when it's their job to reveal the facts."

Don't put your foot in it! Don't put your foot in it!

The second microphone moved in next to the competition. The male reporter asked, "What is your reaction to the Krotch brother's counter suit?"

Ella leaned forward, sticking her tongue out, blowing a raspberry. The female reporter backed up a step.

Garrett said, "That about sums it up." He glanced at Fatima who had her hand over her mouth, eyes open wide.

Kelly laughed. Fatima followed. A camera operator joined in. It spread.

THIRTY-FOUR

<u>Friday, June 27</u>

0

YYC News

<u>Krotch Depravity Caught on Video</u>

By Gwen Chorny

Despite threats of litigation, a video was released today. Kristopher and Harold Krotch, deceased Corporation Mayor Rodney Richardson, and radio personality Giles Patriot appear in the video. Three things of note are depicted in it.

Each of the four men is easily identifiable. Their voices have been verified by forensic voice identification. The four men are shown with a white Charolais calf. The calf performs felatio on each of the men. The men make several in-criminating statements during the video. The most damning is a statement made by Kristopher Krotch when he says, "Boys, we'll make a shitload of money with our bank and realty connections, your little factory, and overall control of the distribution. It's a win win for us all."

The video ends with Harold Krotch putting a handgun to the head of the calf then saying, "Time for some veal!" The next sound is the gun firing, killing the calf.

Later in the video Rodney Richardson says, "Is my insurance policy ready?"

· · · · · · · · · · · · · · · ·

Fatima put the phone down with her left hand. Her right held Ella who had her knees locked around Fatima's waist. "Sanjiv asked if she could see us in half an hour."

Garrett vacuumed up some cereal Ella spilled on the floor. He turned off the vacuum. "What?"

Ella said, "Sanjiv now!"

He leaned the vacuum against a kitchen chair. "How come?"

Fatima said, "Not sure. Can we make it in half an hour?"

Garrett nodded.

Ella said, "Kelly!"

When they opened the door to Sanjiv's office, Ella walked up to Kelly, put her left fist on her hip, lifting the waist of her panties up. "Big girl pants." Kelly got up from behind his desk, putting out his fist, waiting for Ella. She smiled then gave him a fist bump. Kelly picked her up. "I am so proud of you!"

Sanjiv stepped out of her office. "Ella! The star of the hour!"

Ella walked over to Sanjiv to show her she was wearing big girl underwear. Sanjiv nodded at Kelly who waved Garrett and Fatima over to look at his computer monitor. Sanjiv took Ella by the hand, winking at Garrett then walking through the door into Diva Darr's side of the building.

Kelly waited for the door to close, pulling up a window on the monitor. "This just happened." Garrett and Fatima stood on either side of Kelly. He clicked the mouse, putting the video on wide screen. A shot of the Nova Bank in Toronto narrowed into a closer shot of a green Bentley SUV climbing out of underground parking and onto the sidewalk. Cameras, microphones, and reporters swarmed it. A closer shot of a driver behind glass. The horn sounded. No one moved. The driver's window rolled down. Kristopher Krotch had Trump hair, a clean-shaven double chin hanging over the collar of a white shirt and blue tie, and angry blue eyes.

A reporter asked, "Ella Cupola seems unimpressed by your threat of a countersuit. What do you have to say?"

Krotch inhaled, "I fail to understand how that aberration of a child has any insight into complex legal issues." He waved his left hand in dismissal. "She is, like her grandfather, a mere flash in a social media freak circus."

"Asshole." Garrett looked over his shoulder to make sure Ella wasn't within earshot.

Another reporter asked, "Isn't it insensitive to call a toddler an aberration and a freak?"

Krotch's cheeks blossomed red with rage. "Garrett MacGregor's princess of a granddaughter could use a little corporal instruction."

A reporter asked, "Does bovine felatio qualify you to offer advice about child rearing?"

"That video is an unauthenticated fabrication!" The window hummed closed, the horn blared, and the Bentley moved forward as reporters scattered. One was knocked to the ground. The Bentley bumped over the curb, accelerating along Bay Street.

Kelly clicked the mouse and the video shrank. "Ella's video from yesterday has gone viral; it has more hits than the calf video. It's even bigger than the old video of you being hit over the head by Chevrolet."

Fatima said, "I wonder what Jac will think of this?"

"Jac?" Kelly lifted his eyebrows.

"My daughter." Garrett watched as a second video began to play. It showed the Corporation statue of the sausage, videos clips featuring the Krotch brothers, Doug Brown, and Patriot followed by Ella blowing her raspberry. "Holy shit! This is big."

Kelly nodded. "Huge. And it looks like the Krotch brothers and Patriot have gone into hiding."

Sanjiv said, "We've had an offer from the Krotch brothers."

Garrett turned. Ella held a wand in her hand. It was made of clear plastic. The butterfly at the top flashed red, blue, and purple. She said, "Darr gave it to me."

Sanjiv stood behind Ella. Garrett read the concern and bewilderment there. He looked at his granddaughter; realization was a fist on the nose. *She's going to need protecting from the world. Ella's so bright and innocent.*

Sanjiv saw the look, recognizing it. She tried a smile, putting a hand on his shoulder. Garrett shrugged. She said, "She is a gift."

Garrett mumbled. "In so many ways."

They watched her swing the wand and study its colours as it was framed in the window's light.

Garrett asked, "What kind of offer?"

Sanjiv looked over her shoulder at the door to her brother's shop. "Maybe we'd better go into my office." They followed her inside. Kelly followed, closing the door. They sat down around Sanjiv's table.

Ella used her wand to point at the shelf behind Sanjiv's desk where a penis wand lay on its side. "Princess penis?" Laughter erupted. Ella frowned.

Sanjiv said, "The Corporation sausage festival appears to have a life of its own."

Kelly rubbed Ella's back. "We're laughing with you Ella."

Ella turned to Kelly who smiled.

"You tell the best jokes sweetheart." Fatima turned to Sanjiv. "They made an offer?"

Sanjiv nodded, reaching over, taking a blue file from her desk. "Kelly took a call from Toronto this morning. The firm representing the Krotch boys wants to negotiate a settlement with you." She opened the folder and set it on the table. "They also want you to sign an NDA which means you won't be able to reveal the details of the settlement."

Garrett looked at the top of Ella's head. "Is that why Indigo and Hazel were pulled off the job?"

Sanjiv shook her head. "They're still on the job."

Fatima held her palms up, leaning her head to one side as if to say, "What's going on?"

Sanjiv sat back, interlacing her fingers. "They're keeping an eye on Doug Brown and Steve Decker."

Garrett put his hand to his mouth, pointing at Ella's back with his index finger. "Is there reason to worry?"

Sanjiv opened her hands, holding them about six inches apart, shrugging. "Indigo recommended it in case the Krotch boys attempt reprisals. Besides, the CPS has been notified."

Fatima asked, "You mean the police are watching us?"

Sanjiv nodded.

Garrett bounced Ella on his knee. "I have a question about Fatima's insurance company. How did you get them to do a one-eighty and pay Fatima's claim?"

Sanjiv glanced at Kelly. "I just told them I had evidence proving you and Fatima were being falsely accused of, among other things, arson. A lawsuit in such a high profile case would cost them more than a settlement."

Fatima raised her eyebrows, looking at Garrett as if to say, "I told you she's good."

Sanjiv tapped a manicured forefinger on the open file. "It's my job to present this offer to you."

Ella said, "Okay."

Sanjiv smiled at Ella then looked at the file. "There are several aspects to the settlement. One is the NDA. The second is an agreement for them to publish a retraction in *Upper Canada Press* and three is a monetary settlement."

"A retraction buried in the want ads?" Garrett asked.

Sanjiv said, "So far the Krotch's maintain that placement of the retraction is within their purview."

Fatima asked, "So far?"

Sanjiv smiled. "This is their opening bid. You can counter."

Ella leaned forward to put her elbows on the table. Garrett said, "So we keep out mouths shut, and they print a retraction somewhere in UCP. That's it?"

"And ten thousand dollars." Sanjiv raised her eyebrows.

Ella put her tongue between her lips and blew.

Fatima said, "Karah alaikum."

Garrett shrugged. "I think Ella and Fatima summed it up. Shit on them."

Sanjiv laughed. "I was hoping you'd say that. This new video of the Krotch boys has become a cause célèbre. I have some ideas for a counter offer."

THIRTY-FIVE

<u>Saturday, June 28</u>

O

YYC News

<u>Krotch Video Draws Universal Revulsion</u>

The video of the Krotch brothers having felatio performed on them by a calf and the subsequent execution of the calf has resulted in revulsion from a number of organizations and groups.

PETA (People for the Ethical Treatment of Animals) has announced its intention of demonstrating in front of Nova Bank headquarters in Toronto.

The Humane Society of Canada is calling for the arrest of the brothers on a charge of cruelty to animals. Reactions to the video have *come from around the globe.*

An unexpected development is that Ella Cupola has become a social media phenomenon. The video of Garrett MacGregor's eighteen-month-old granddaughter is predicted to surpass ten million views by the end of the weekend.

Kristopher Krotch's derogatory remarks about toddler Ella Cupola have intensified the negative responses to the Krotch brothers, as well as the calls to boycott their bank, media, and real estate operations.

· · · · · · · · · · · · · · · ·

Jac struggled to keep an even tone as she asked, "Can we come over now? We need to talk."

About what? "Sure come over." Garrett hung up the phone. He looked around his condo. Dayna and Fatima were at the dressmaker's.

He looked out the window, then dialed David's number.

"What's up Dad?"

"Jacolynne just phoned, and she's coming right over. Any idea what's up?"

"Sure. You know her crazy friend Carole?"

"The one who's born again and married to the accountant? The one with the perfect child? The one who made herself feel better by making Jac feel second best all the way through high school?" Garrett leaned his back up against the counter.

"Jac and Ella went over there last night. It was supposed to be a play date with Carole's daughter, Angel. Apparently things didn't go well. Ella talked in complete sentences and recently potty trained herself. Angel, on the other hand, shit her pants and has a ten-word vocabulary. Carole was pissed right off, took it out on Ella who told her, and I quote, 'Get over yourself.'"

Garrett laughed. "Carole always was kind of nasty to Jac."

"And Jac never wanted to hear it from us."

"How are you doing?"

"Better. Let me know how it goes."

"Okay." Garrett heard David hang up.

The doorbell rang several times. He opened the door. Ella walked in followed by Jac and Mark. Mark wore seventy-hour work week fatigue. Ella's runners sparkled. Garrett asked, "Want a coffee Mark?"

Mark said, "Love one."

Ella headed for the grapes and crackers Garrett had put

on the table. Jacolynne stuck her head in the fridge, pulling out an apple. She closed the door, rinsing the apple in the sink while Garrett went to the espresso machine to make a couple of lattes. He set a cup in front of David who sat on the couch next to Jac. Garrett sat in an armchair, closing his eyes just to feel the sun on his face, sipping his latte. Ella brought a hand full of crackers over and sat on her dad's lap.

Garrett set his coffee down. "What's up?"

Jac looked at Mark, sipping his latte while leaning away from Ella to prevent a hot spill. Ella said, "Carole called me a freak." She nibbled on one side of the cracker, snuggling up under Mark's arm.

Garrett leaned forward, feeling the heat on his face.

Jac chewed on apple, covering her mouth. "Ella said Angel was stinky."

Ella held her nose.

Mark shook his head. "Why is this such a big deal?"

Jac turned to him. "Because I'm worried about our daughter. She's potty trained, she speaks in complete sentences, her vocabulary seems to be expanding exponentially, and she's way ahead of other kids twice her age."

Mark asked, "Why's that such a bad thing?"

The door opened. Dayna walked in followed by Fatima. "Are we interrupting?"

Jac shook her head, Mark smiled, and Ella said, "Carole says I'm a freak."

Fatima shut the door, mumbling something under her breath.

Dayna looked at Jac. "Who is Carole?"

Jac shrugged. "An old friend."

Mark stood up, taking his cup to the sink. "Carole thinks her Angel is perfect, and our Ella is a freak. She's always had this competitive streak."

Fatima asked, "Is this Angel an angel?"

Ella lifted the sleeve of her right bicep to reveal an angry red oval. "No. She bit me."

Dayna leaned her head to the right. Puzzlement appeared in her eyes. "Ella's vocabulary is a problem? And Carole is mad because Ella has a vocabulary?"

Mark leaned against the counter. "Go figure."

Dayna picked Ella up, then said, "Aren't friends supposed to be nice to their friend's kids?"

Garrett thought, *If anyone else had said that, Jacolynne would have bristled, but she listens to Dayna.*

Jac's face reddened. She stood up, walking over to Dayna and Ella. "Yes."

Dayna kissed Ella on the cheek. "Shouldn't friends congratulate rather than criticize?"

Jac rubbed Ella's back. Her voice sounded tired. "Yes."

Fatima said, "I remember this Carole." She opened her mouth to say more then closed it.

Jac looked at her. "What?"

Fatima shook her head.

Ella pointed half a cracker at Fatima. "What?"

Fatima looked at Garrett then said, "This child is a gift. I'm sorry but this Carole is the problem, not Ella."

Dayna said, "Mom just picked up her wedding dress, and she looks amazing."

Jac kissed her daughter on the cheek.

Ella pointed at Fatima. "I picked out the ring."

THIRTY-SIX

<u>Sunday, June 29</u>

0

"Hey it's Riley. You got a minute?"

Garrett talked on his cell as he walked from his condo to Fatima's house. He'd been told to bring his camera. He crossed the field east of Queen Mary High School. "Go ahead."

"It's all set. The wedding is happening at eleven thirty. If possible, we'd like you there at eight to enjoy the breakfast and parade. After the wedding is lunch. We don't know how many people will be there so we don't want to call it a reception. We don't know what to call it except lunch. I hope you and Fatima don't mind."

"I'm just on my way to see the kids trying on their dresses and tuxes. I'm supposed to take pictures. I'll ask Fatima. Can you text me or email the schedule of events just so I can show her?" Garrett passed into the shade of trees towering three stories above him into an impossibly blue prairie sky.

"Sure. No problem."

"How are things on your end?"

Riley chuckled. "Crazy. Got the sculpture done at midnight last night. It's on a flatbed. Sam's phone has been going non-stop since before seven this morning with last minute details and questions. I don't know how he keeps all the people and events straight in his head. There's this quirky Toronto food critic coming. Her name is Miriam Webley. She expects Corporation to have a five star hotel! Wait 'til she has to choose between the old hotel or the no tell motel. I'd pay money to see her reaction."

"Who does she work for?"

"She travels the world and has her own TV show called Miriam's Gastronome Guide."

Garrett had a vision of Miriam with a two thousand dollar purse, white gloves, designer dress, and stiletto heels traversing one of Corporation's unpaved roads. "Are the drag queens coming?"

"More than twenty are arriving on a yellow and black bus they call The Hive."

Garrett grinned. "Your rat rod friends gonna be there?"

"You betcha. Each one will have a drag queen as a passenger for the parade. Should be fun."

Garrett looked ahead at Fatima's bungalow shaded by the leaves of her poplar tree. "How about Doug Brown? What's he up to?"

"That's another funny thing. You remember Steve Decker?"

"Yes."

Riley took a breath. "He seems to like it here. Anyway, he was walking his dog on Main Street. He stopped and talked with me. Said that Brown left town. Went east for some job."

"That's good."

"Good for us because Brown's gone. Sydney, Jean, and Gwen all said he gave them the creeps."

"I wonder what he's up to down east?"

Riley took a moment. "I wonder if we'll ever know."

Garrett zigzagged through an opening in the schoolyard fence. "Right now all I know is Jac, Dayna, and Ella are trying their dresses on for the wedding. Mark and David are in tuxes."

"Better let you go. See you Tuesday."

"See you then." Garrett stuffed the phone in his shirt pocket, crossing the street, walking up Fatima's front sidewalk, going around the side of the house, and opening the gate.

Jac said, "Ella! Dayna needs those!"

Garrett saw Ella run toward the neighbour's fence. She wore white shoes, a mauve dress, and carried a white flower basket with a candy cane handle.

"Ella!" Jac made a grab for her daughter, missing when Ella dodged left.

Ella reached into her basket, flinging a flesh couloured disc out. It floated to the ground. Jac bent to pick it up. Ella stopped, reaching for a second disc. She cocked her arm, tossing the disc. It floated up onto the roof of the garage.

"What is that?" Garrett knew the answer when the words left his lips.

Jac said, "Boob enhancers."

Ella laughed. "Boobs!"

Jac turned to her father. "Can you watch her while we finish?"

"Sure." He walked over to his granddaughter, scooping her up, ducking when she swung the basket. It missed his forehead, but one corner caught the top of his head. Garrett set her down, taking the basket with one hand, rubbing his head with the other. "Okay if I sit down for a minute?" Ella shook her head, running across the grass.

Mark came out the back door. He wore a black tux, white shirt, and black shoes. "What's Ella up to?"

Garrett pointed at the garage roof. "She threw a boob on the roof."

David followed Mark out the door. He was dressed the same as his brother-in-law. He looked at Ella. "Where's the boob?"

She pointed at the garage roof.

Garrett opened the garage door. "There's a ladder in here." He switched on the light, lifting the ladder off the wall. David grabbed one end of the ladder. They maneuvered it above Fatima's vintage white BMW motorcycle and out the door. Mark held a squirming Ella while Garrett and David set the ladder up against the garage roof. David looked at his tux and shoes. Garrett said, "I'll go." He pulled his camera out of his pants pocket, setting it on the table, going back to the ladder, and climbing onto the roof. He crabbed over the asphalt shingles, picking up the flesh coloured gell disc, and starting back.

"What are you doing on the roof?"

He looked down, seeing Fatima standing with her left hand on her hip, and her right shading her eyes. *You look great!* "Just getting a boob." Garrett climbed half way down the ladder and turned. He wiggled the gell boob between his thumb and forefinger, looking at Fatima. "Is this yours?"

She took it from him, holding it against her right breast. "No, but I think I know who's missing it." Fatima went back into the house.

David put his hand on his father's shoulder. "You know what? Life's still never boring when you're around."

Mark laughed. Ella joined in, and had them all going until Jac, Siobhan, Dayna, and Fatima came outside. Fatima still wore her blue blouse, white shorts, and sandals. Jac wore a pale blue off the shoulder number, stunning Mark into silence. Siobhan wore a strapless red satin dress and Dayna a black tux, red shirt, and black shorts. Garrett smiled.

David said, "Holy shit!"

Fatima directed the pictures she wanted taken. There were frequent interruptions for Ella and for everyone to run around, take pee breaks, and then iced tea breaks. Garrett found himself getting into the rhythm of taking photographs, capturing candid moments, and listening to the chatter of his family.

Dayna tucked her hand inside her jacket in a Napoleonic pose. "Mom!"

Fatima turned to her. "We need pictures of you and Garrett."

Garrett had a flashback of his first wedding. The pictures of Marie who wore white, had polished white teeth, and a painted on smile. Marie had planned everyone's wardrobe down to the shoelaces. Someone had kept saying in his ear, "Happy wife. Happy life." Then he looked at Fatima's smile and how she'd let the boys choose their own tuxes, the girls their own dresses. *Fatima's wedding is all about everyone else.* The thought struck him, a palm flat against the sternum. He staggered.

Jac asked, "Dad? You okay?"

He looked at her, discovering he couldn't answer.

"Dad?" David asked.

Fatima took his elbow. "You okay?"

He shrugged, kissing her on the lips. She tasted of iced tea, cherry lip balm, and last night's garlic. Garrett closed his eyes, savouring her and this delicious moment.

· · · · · · · · · · · · · · ·

YYC News
<u>BREAKING NEWS</u>

Members of the RCMP's O Division have descended upon a property at Port Warwick, Ontario.

The RCMP operation used boats, a helicopter, and ground vehicles to surround a property owned by Kristopher Krotch, a member of one of Canada's wealthiest families and director of the Nova Bank. Early reports are that Mr. Krotch was not on site, but several other men were taken into custody.

An RCMP spokesperson said, "More detailed infor-mation will be released at this afternoon's press conference."

. . . .

Garrett's phone rang, vibrating against his ribs. He pulled the phone out of his shirt pocket, reading the name. "What's up Sanjiv?" He sat in Fatima's back yard. Ella was asleep on a blanket in the shade of the garage. The kids were getting changed into casual clothes. Fatima was downloading pictures onto her computer.

"I got a call from the Krotch brothers' lawyers."

"Don't you get a day off?"

"I gave them my number just in case. Anyway, they have made a substantial improvement to their offer."

"How come?" Garrett watched Ella's gentle breathing, smiling as she rolled onto her back.

"Have you been following the news?"

Garrett frowned. "No, what's happened?"

"The RCMP raided a Krotch property in Ontario. Unconfirmed reports indicate they seized a large cache of weapons and several million dollars worth of cocaine."

"Don't those guys have enough money?"

Sanjiv chuckled. "Apparently not. I think the Krotch lawyers want to get us out of the way. This thing is blowing up in their faces. It may be too late for damage control, because it looks like this Krotch thing hit a critical mass. The video of the calf had people upset. Today's news will add weight to our case. Is there any way you and Fatima can come in tomorrow morning?"

"Sure. I've got to swing by Rowan's at ten to pick up the rings."

"Ten-thirty okay?"

Garrett nodded. "See you then."

THIRTY-SEVEN

<u>Monday, June 30</u>

O

Garrett closed his eyes, feeling the wind against his face, opening them to watch the tourquoise Bow River flow east and south. He sat next to Fatima in the sidecar of her motorcycle. He thought about their first date and how she'd driven him to Inglewood on a Friday night. He smiled as she turned left, following a side street, and pulling up front of Deva Darr's.

He hoisted himself up. They both took off their helmets, stuffing them in the nose of the sidecar. Fatima took off her red leather jacket, setting it on the seat. "I need to talk with Darr for a minute." She pointed her thumb at the door to the brick building.

Garrett pointed east. "I'll be right back. Rowan's got the rings ready." He walked the sidewalk under mature trees, passing hundred-year-old houses, and more modern infills. He turned up the walk to Rowan's Jewellers, and inside the two-storey, nineteen twenties shop with the creaky-oak-floors. Rowan stood next to a glass display case, stroking his black beard. "Good morning. It's all ready for you." He reached over, pulling two boxes from a drawer. He set the boxes atop a black velvet cloth on the display case glass. "Please take a look."

Garrett smiled, leaning over the case. "Thanks for getting them done on such short notice."

Rowan opened the boxes, setting the white gold rings on the black. "I think you will be pleased."

Garrett looked closely at his plain white gold band and Fatima's Baguette ring with the diamonds set inside. He looked at Rowan, smiling while pulling out his credit card. Ten minutes later he walked into Deva Darr's. Darr was dressed in red. "Here's the groom!"

Darr had this way of moving, or rather floating. *How the hell does he do that?*

"You think my sister's the only dancer in the family?" Darr put his arm around Garrett's shoulder.

Another person can read my mind. That's just great!

Darr pinched Garrett's cheek. "I love that face of yours, because it's so damned transparent!"

"This is my poker face!"

"Well then, if that's your poker face you'd better stay the hell outta Vegas!"

"Garrett?" Fatima stepped out from behind the door to the law office. "Sanjiv has some news for us."

Darr gave him a quick shove. Garrett walked to the open door then into Sanjiv's reception area. Kelly handed him a cup of coffee and a smile as he followed Fatima into Sanjiv's office. She sat at the table with papers in front of her. There were red stickers pointing at sections in documents. Sanjiv was eating a bagel and sipping an orange juice. Her hair was tied back. She wore a white blouse and blue scarf. She covered her mouth. "Please sit."

Garrett sat down. Fatima sat next to him. He took a sip of his coffee, sensing the expectancy in the room. "You're feeling better."

Sanjiv grabbed a white napkin. "Yes, thank you, and I'm craving orange juice." She took a sip. "I think I have some good news, that is besides the fact tomorrow's your wedding. Congratulations by the way." She pointed at the documents in front of her. "Kelly put these together this morning just in case. The Krotch boys have matched our–" She pointed at Garrett. "–your proposal."

He did some quick mental math. "What?"

Fatima put her hand on his arm. "You're joking!"

Sanjiv shook her head. "It appears their recent difficulties have put them in the mood to settle."

Garrett sat back, looking at Fatima who was staring at the documents as if they might rise off the desk and burst into flame.

"Their lawyer has agreed to have the cheque in my hands by closing today if I have the signed documents to him by 2:00 PM Toronto time."

"So my kids will have their mortgages paid off?" he asked.

"That's correct. It's the first thing to be done after the cheque is verified."

"And the apology will be on the front page?" Fatima asked.

"Page two." Sanjiv held a piece of bagel in the air, raising her eyebrows.

"And?" Garrett asked.

"Three point five million–" She popped the bagel bit into her mouth. "–plus expenses."

Garrett looked at Fatima whose eyes were filling with tears. He asked, "What's the matter?"

"You still want to get married?" She put her hand over her mouth.

Garrett leaned his head to the left, opening his hands. "Are you joking?" He heard Sanjiv inhale. It sounded like a whimper.

Fatima shook her head. "You're a millionaire now."

He shrugged, looking at Sanjiv. He read the disbelief in her eyes. *How could such good news turn out like this?* Garrett pointed at his lawyer. "Do you know yesterday we had the kids over for pictures? They all had outfits chosen by them, but paid for by Fatima." He turned to her. "You're the bride, and your biggest concern is if everyone else is going to have a good time."

Fatima reached for a tissue.

Garrett shrugged. "I have a family now. A real family. Who in his right mind would throw that away?"

Fatima said, "I just thought... I mean. You might want to think about. You know."

Garrett shook his head. "I want to get married tomorrow, to you, in Corporation, at the Canada Day Sausage Festival. If you'll have me." *Somehow that doesn't sound quite the way it sounded in my mind.*

Sanjiv laughed first.

Half an hour later after the papers had been signed, and Sanjiv said she'd call when the cheque arrived and cleared. Garrett stretched his feet out, kicking a plastic bag stuffed into the nose of the sidecar. He looked up at Fatima who was concentrating on a minivan with a habit of changing lanes without signaling. He looked back down at the bag. A red box fell out. The label read `Lady Minerva Enhancers'. He stuffed the box back into the bag as the breeze off the Bow River caressed his cheek.

THIRTY-EIGHT

Tuesday, July 1

0

YYC News
BREAKING NEWS

The OPP and RCMP have closed the southbound lanes of Highway 401 between London and Windsor. Police are in pursuit of a green Bentley SUV.

RCMP spokesperson Constable Kelly Ryder said, "The Bentley was ordered to stop as it approached Pearson Airport. It drove away at high speed. Officers called for air support when public safety was deemed at risk."

Ryder would not comment on reports the occupants of the Bentley are billionaire brothers Kristopher and Harold Krotch.

. . . .

The early morning Rockies were painted a darker shade of pink in the west. A few peaks were tipped with snow. Garrett sat in the passenger's seat of his Ford while David drove north and west of Calgary on Highway 22. Ahead, Jac drove their Tiguan and out front of them, Dayna drove Fatima's Ford Escape.

David had his music playing–a mixture of rap, techno, and

folk. Garrett kept an eye on the cars ahead.

David asked, "Nervous?"

Garrett did an internal check for butterflies. "A bit."

"Just remember you and Fatima need to have fun today."

Garrett nodded. "Thanks."

"What's the matter? You're very quiet."

"Just thinking."

David lifted his chin. "There are some more rat rods." He pointed at a pair of vehicles with rust patina finishes. One looked vaguely from the nineteen fifties and the other–with a rumble seat–might have had its origins in the nineteen thirties. Both had low slung frames and open wheels. They pulled over onto the shoulder. Garrett waved as they passed. David asked, "How many is that?"

Garrett shrugged. "Maybe thirty. It's like being in some post apocalyptic movie where everyone drives cars made from bits and pieces." He looked ahead. "There's another pickup towing a horse trailer. There've been lots of those too."

"This is the first time I've ever seen the traffic get heavier when we get closer to Corporation."

"The insurance company say anything about your Jeep?"

David lifted his cast. "They said I could keep the rental for a month because of this." He held up his casted arm. "Then you want to come with me to pick out a new one? I'm covered for a replacement vehicle."

"Think we can get the same salesman?"

"You mean the Thunder Down Under?" They laughed at the memory of the Australian reality star who'd sold them the first Jeep.

Ten kilometers further along, they turned east onto a gravel road then up over some railway tracks. Five minutes after that, they pulled into Riley and Sam's yard south and east of Corporation. The two storey cream-coloured house Garrett's grandparents had ordered from a catalogue and built in the twenties greeted them. Across from the house was the red Quonset where Riley spent his winters creating. A yellow and black bus, with THE HIVE written along its side, was parked between the barn and chicken coop.

David parked next to the Quonset, Dayna and Jac in front of the house. As they climbed out of their vehicles, the door to the garage opened. A silver Ford diesel pickup clattered as it backed out. Sam waved from behind the wheel. He rolled down his window, pointing at Fatima. "Go on inside. The house is yours!" He steered the truck over in front of the Quonset, backing it up to the closed overhead door. He shut the truck off and stepped out. He wore jeans and a black T-shirt. He offered his hand to Garrett then grabbed and hugged him. "Want to see Riley's masterpiece?" Sam gestured Garrett to follow as he went up to the side door. Inside Garrett waited for his eyes to adjust. A fifty foot pink sausage leaned its tip over the front end of a gooseneck trailer. The neck of the trailer wore a red and white Excalibur Trailer decal.

Sam pressed a button. The overhead door opened. "Can you guide me?"

Garrett waited for Sam to climb into the truck then stood where Sam could see him in the side mirror. The pickup inched backwards. Garrett brought his hands together as the distance to the hitch closed. When his hands met, Sam stopped, and climbed out. "Looks good. I'll get this outta here so you guys'll have a place to change." Sam lowered the trailer onto the hitch then moved the truck, trailer, and sculpture out into the yard. Garrett went inside the Quonset, pressing the button to close the overhead door. He looked over at the yellow bus where a queen with red hair, a silver ball gown, and red stilletos stepped down onto a red outdoor carpet.

Garrett went to the side door, almost running into David and Mark who carried their tuxes inside. David said, "We gotta hurry. We're supposed to be there in thirty minutes."

They hung the tuxes on hooks. Then they set the shirts, shoes, ties, and socks on the table Riley had set up.

Garrett began to undo the buttons on his shirt. He inhaled the mixture of dust, compost, diesel, grease, and mice. He closed his eyes at the memory of his white-haired grandfather. The man with hands the size of dinner plates who worked until the second last day of his life. Grandpa's words came back to him as they stood inside the shop after Garrett's mother had told him to go play outside so she could take his brothers into the city for new shoes. He and his grandfather had spent some time gathering eggs, then they went to the shop inside the Quonset to work on a project. Garrett tried to remember the project. Instead he remembered his grandfather's words, "Shit happens in life. You have to learn to get over it and get on with living."

He put on his blue shirt. Next came the black pants for the tux. He looked at the concrete floor, smiling at the ten-foot square of green outdoor carpet Riley had rolled out for them. The red skater shoes had been Fatima's idea. He smiled at the cushioned inserts.

Mark was putting on his jacket. David had a short-sleeved shirt on, fumbling with the buttons. He looked at his father, raising his eyebrows. Garrett smiled then reached for David's tie. He slipped the silk off his son's neck, put it around his own, standing in front of the four-foot antique mirror. He tied a Windsor, slipping it up and over his head, then pulling it over David's, and turning the collar down.

There was a knock at the door. Riley stepped inside. He wore a grey suit. *I didn't know that he owned a suit.* Riley said, "Ready to go?" He pointed at David and Mark. "Okay if you two ride with Sam and you–" He pointed at Garrett. "–ride with me?"

Garrett grabbed his tie, pulling on his jacket, following David and Mark outside.

David said, "Shotgun!" and ran for the silver Ford.

Sam wore a navy blue suit. He climbed behind the wheel. Mark climbed in the back seat.

Garrett looked left as The Hive's diesel hummed to life. "Climb in!" Riley pointed at his red vintage Ford pickup.

Riley eased up behind the trailer. Garrett peered up the inside of the shaft of the fifty-foot sausage then turned to look behind. The Hive stopped out front of Riley and Sam's house. Dayna appeared on the back step, waving Sam and Garrett to move ahead. Riley said, "She wants you to be surprised when you see Fatima." He beeped the horn. Sam rolled the truck and sculpture ahead along the driveway to the main road. About three minutes later, The Hive pulled up behind Riley's truck, and they headed for town.

Riley watched the sausage as it rocked and bounced on the trailer. "I hope it doesn't break."

Garrett raised his eyebrows, looking at his cousin who smiled. "No jokes, please I've already heard them all!"

"Can I just say, it's bigger than I remember?"Garrett adjusted his tie. "Thanks for doing all of this."

"You're kidding right?"

"No." Garrett shrugged.

Riley shook his head. "We asked you to help us out. The media slammed you, Fatima's place got torched, and you had to hire bodyguards. We are happy to be able to pay you all back."

They approached the paved highway. Garrett pointed. "What the hell is that?"

Riley looked north. Traffic was backed up all the way to Corporation, which was two kilometers further along the road. "I think it's a traffic jam. That's a first."

"Are we going to be late?"

Riley pulled a cell phone from the inner pocket of his jacket. "Sydney said to call if we had any trouble."

Five minutes later, an RCMP cruiser with lights flashing, and siren howling escorted the wedding convoy past the two-kilometre lineup of trucks, cars, vintage automobiles, motorcycles, and rat rods. The escort led them to the south end of town and the north side of the lake. They joined another lineup of vintage cars, trucks, and a blue eight-wheeled tractor towing a rainbow float.

Sam got out of his truck with an iPad under his arm, pointing at Riley. "You get up there and–" He pointed at Garrett. "–you keep your eyes looking north. And don't cheat in the mirror." He looked at his iPad, tapping the screen.

Garrett asked, "What's he doing?"

Riley released the clutch, easing them up the road toward the hotel. "He's got it all organized on his iPad; who rides on the float, who rides in what car."

Garrett inhaled, letting the breath out slow. "Is he okay doing all of this work?"

"Are you kidding? He's in his glory."

Five minutes later, Sam walked up to Riley's truck. "I'm gonna pull ahead of you, then you follow along until we end up at the fair grounds." He pointed at his truck. David and Mark climbed out, went to the rear of Riley's truck, standing behind the cab. Sam went back to the silver Ford. He and the fifty-foot pink shaft led the way up to the hotel, then turned right onto Main Street.

Garrett noticed the sidewalk on either side of the paved road was lined with people standing or sitting in lawn chairs. They waved with their hands or the plastic sausage wands Garrett recognized from Sanjiv's office. Colours flashed up the handles to the tips. He checked for anyone having a seizure, seeing smiles instead. Riley tapped his knuckles on the roof. "Throw the candy!"

Mark and David reached into the bucket. They tossed lollipops out either side. Kids scrambled as the candies bounced off pavement.

A camera crew filmed from the back of a pickup parked at the corner near the Co-Op.

A woman squatted next to a doublewide orange stroller, pointing so her children could see the float. The man standing next to her caught a lollipop, handing it to the mom. She unwrapped it, passing it to one child. The other howled until another lollipop was tossed.

Garrett turned to Riley. "How many people are here?"

Riley shook his head. "Don't know. Just hope we have enough food."

Dance music pounded. The crowd roared. Riley checked the side mirror. He turned to Garrett. "Some of the drag queens are dancing on the float. They're pointing at the cowboys and inviting them up. There goes one guy! And another!"

Garrett spotted someone behind the window of the barbershop. A woman stood there. She wore white and had her arms crossed; a reflection within a reflection.

He looked ahead. A police truck blocked a side street. The officer leaned against the front fender. He recognized Sydney and waved. She smiled, nodding. Three boys sat cross-legged on the roof of the truck. A man with strawberry blond hair stood behind them in the box of the truck.

David tossed lollipops to the boys.

Luke walked along the sidewalk shooting candids.

In the next block, a woman sat in a lawn chair in the shade of a tree. She was surrounded by what appeared to be her children and grandchildren. Riley tapped the horn then pointed right. "There's Jean!" Garrett waved. Jean smiled, standing, pointing, and saying something to her family who waved.

Sam did a right turn. They drove past Corporation's monument to the sausage. It bore a fresh coat of beige and brown paint from where it rose up between two spruce trees sculpted into globes. A crowd of people sat on blankets and lawn chairs. Kids ran across the grass to gather up lollipops tossed their way. Sam did a left. Garrett looked north. The radio station was still there, but the two-storey billboard of Giles Patriot was gone. "What happened to Patriot's sign?"

"He went into hiding. Some of us decided the sign could be used for kindling." Riley pointed. "We're almost there."

Garrett spotted the church spire ahead; it was a white stuccoed, green-roofed building with stained glass windows on either side. Riley stopped out front, the boys hopping out the back. Luke waited with his camera. Garrett heard the shutter clicking. Riley put his hand on Garrett's shoulder. "Sam's gonna park at the fair grounds. I'm gonna give him a ride back. We'll be back in a minute." Garrett climbed out. He closed the door, looking at David and Mark waiting at the foot of the steps to the church. The double church doors opened. A boy in a white cassock said, "Father Shane told me to bring you to the sacristy." The boy led the way up the stairs, holding the door for them. He went between the pews before turning right at the altar and opening an oak door. Garrett walked through to be greeted by a priest whose vestments were almost as white as his teeth.

He held out his hand, shaking each of theirs in turn. "I'm Father Shane. We usually hold a rehearsal. You understand this is a personal favour for Riley MacGregor?"

Where is this going? "Okay." Garrett felt his face redden.

Shane asked, "And I understand there may be some unusual guests attending the ceremony?"

David coughed into the elbow of his casted arm. "We're all pretty unusual."

Mark looked sideways at his brother-in-law. "Some more than others."

Shane nodded. "I'll get you three to wait in here while I

prepare for the service." He stepped out.

David lifted his eyebrows. "He's kind of intense."

Mark looked at Garrett. "You ever been to this place before?"

Garrett nodded. "Used to come here on Sunday mornings with my grandfather. There would be prayers in German before mass started."

David tilted his head back. "I thought he was Scotch."

"He was but a lot of the other farmers were German by way of Russia." Garrett looked out the window, seeing the tail end of the parade, a pair of rat rods followed by a Model T.

The organ started up. The door opened and a different altar boy said, "Follow me." He led the way out to the front of the altar.

Garrett, Mark, and David stopped when the altar boy pointed at a black tile in the white floor. "Stand there."

This feels like a military operation. Garrett looked around him. He noticed the oak pews down either side of the main aisle; the stained glass windows; the choir loft above the font entrance where a red-haired lady played the organ; the altar.

The front doors opened. Fatima's mother and father looked around, following the usher up the aisle. They'd just returned from a year in Lebanon caring for her aged mother. She wore a black dress and smiled at Garrett. The father wore a black suit and gave a small wave. More of Fatima's cousins, aunts, uncles, customers, a few former inlaws, and friends followed.

David opened the corner of his mouth nearest to his father. "Are you okay that your brothers aren't here?"

"Relieved actually." *They would find a way to ruin this.*

In a matter of five minutes, the church was nearly full except for the last two rows, and a few spots up front. Riley and Sam arrived, waved, and sat near the back.

About half the people are Fatima's family and friends and the other half I don't recognize. Then he noticed Jean, Gwen, and Sydney sitting with a dark-haired woman of about forty or fifty who wore white. *She looks like the woman in the barbershop window.* It must be Melvin's wife Cathy.

The organist played *Here Comes the Bride*. The double doors opened. Ella walked up the aisle in her mauve dress, carrying a white basket. She locked eyes on Garrett. Someone said, "Throw the flowers."

Ella reached into her basket and lifted a round, flesh coloured petal the size of a saucer. She flipped it to her right. It flew up and over the heads of the guests. She took another between her thumb and forefinger. This one went left, slapping a boy of seventeen or eighteen on the side of the face.

Garrett remembered the red packages of Lady Minerva Enhancers stuffed in the nose of Fatima's sidecar. Ella tossed another. This time someone caught it. "These aren't flower petals they're..." The last word was muffled by a woman's hand over a man's mouth.

Ella tossed another. A murmur rippled though the crowd.

Luke's camera flashed as twenty drag queens led by Deva Dave–wearing a white wedding gown complete with veil–followed Ella up the aisle. The queens' hair was blonde, brunette, and red along with beehives of purple and pink. The dresses were all ball gowns except for Darr's. No two gowns were the same colour, each its own masterpiece. The queens balanced on twenty pairs of stilletos. They parted, sitting on either side in the last four rows.

He saw Fatima in a silver white gown. Her bare arms held a bouquet of roses. Her red hair settled on her shoulders. She smiled at Garrett. He closed his mouth, smiling back. He heard a rustling and some exclamations when heads turned to see Fatima and Dayna in her tux half way up the aisle and closing. Fatima took his hand. Jac, Siobhan, and Ella stood to one side. The priest began to speak.

Ella sat down on the step, looking at the people in the front row. Garrett saw a smudge of choclate on her cheek. He glanced at Fatima's mother Fermita who was gesturing at Ella who shook her head no. Garrett thought, *I hope someone told her about our potty training deal.*

Fermita frowned, leaning forward with a white handkerchief.

Ella's chin dropped.

Oh, oh. That's a bad sign.

Ella said, "Back off Jedda, or I'll shit my big girl panties!"

Luke's camera flash accentuated the remark.

Jac's face blushed. She leaned over to pull Ella to her feet.

Garrett heard a few chuckles in the crowd, especially from the drag queens. He saw Fermita's jaw set.

Ella looked up at the priest. "Are you God?"

Garrett heard a gasp from the back of the church.

Ella leaned forward, tugging at David's pants. "Daddy? Where's God?"

Garrett turned when someone near the back cried out. He wasn't sure if it was a sob or a laugh. He saw Sydney turning to the dark haired woman in white. Cathy Gartner's eyes looked at the ceiling, her mouth wide open. She laughed. Sydney smiled. Jean leaned forward, laughing. The first row of drag queens roared. Laughter spread up and down the rows. Garrett looked at Jac. Ella pointed at the crucifix. Fatima rubbed the child's back. There was a bark to Garrett's left. He saw the priest leaning forward, laughter shaking his shoulders. He lifted his face as tears rolled down his cheeks.

Now that is a surprise.

Fatima put her hand on Garrett's shoulder, then put her mouth to his ear. "Isn't this perfect?" She touched her lips to his cheek.

• • • • • • • • • • • • • • •

YYC News

<u>BREAKING NEWS</u>

RCMP Inspector Mary Ruryk confirmed Kristopher and Harold Krotch were apprehended after a high-speed chase. The pursuit caused closures of sections of the 401 highway between London and Windsor, Ontario.

Ruryk said, "The pair were arrested after the Bentley passed over a spike belt, and the vehicle collided with a safety barrier. Both occupants were unharmed and taken into custody."

Inspector Ruryk added, "Kristopher and Harold Krotch will appear in court tomorrow. They will be facing a series of charges."

Confirmed reports indicate the Krotch brothers' private jet was on standby at Windsor International Airport. The pilot had not filed a flightplan and is being interviewed by Windsor police.

• • • • • • • • • • • • • • •

Garrett and Fatima stood on the sidewalk in front of the church where an informal line of well wishers waited to shake their hands, kiss their cheeks, take a selfie, or get a closer look at Ella. The line thinned. Fatima was in an animated conversation in Arabic with her mother. He couldn't tell if they were arguing or catching up. He looked at the lawn where Ella sat. She wore a crown one of the queens had given her. Jac and Mark sat on either side of her. Cathy Gartner and Jean crouched down to get eye to eye with Ella. Garrett walked over, getting down on one knee next to Mark.

Cathy turned to Ella. "I wanted to thank you."

Jac patted the grass. "Come and sit."

Cathy sat down, closing her eyes, lifting her face to the sun. "I never thought I would do that again."

"What?" Ella asked.

Cathy leaned forward to wrap her arms around her knees. "Laugh. You made me laugh for the first time in a long time."

Luke crouched in front of them. The camera whirred.

Ella nodded, puzzled.

Cathy looked at Jac. "Thank you for raising a child who is free to ask questions. I think I'll ask more questions from now on."

Jac nodded, putting an arm around Ella who was distracted by a dragonfly. "Thank you."

Garrett looked at Jean, seeing tears at the corners of her eyes. She smiled at Garrett while pulling a tissue from her sleeve.

Sam pulled up in his silver truck. "Come on, you're late for the reception!"

Garrett opened the door, helping Fatima into the front seat of the cab. Jac, Siobhan, Ella, and Dayna got in the back seat. Garrett and the boys climbed in the box. Jean and Cathy hopped up, sitting on the tailgate. Sam drove west, turning north where four baseball diamonds backed up against the arena. The bleachers faced the corral. Food stands, trucks, barbecues, and trailers gathered in front of the backstops in a rough square. In the arena, a red tractor pulled a crumbler roller to level and compact the earth. An announcer's booth sat balanced on six poles. The base of the booth was four metres of planks flanked by speakers. Coffee shop umbrellas shaded the announcers. A rainbow flag flapped above them. Beyond the booth sat the fifty-foot sausage on its trailer, with a yellow mobile crane beside.

Sam pulled up, parking next to the sausage. In front of them a row of food stands: Sausage Rolls, King of Kolbasa, Polish Sausage, Best Sausage, Chorizo Heaven, Footlong Peckeroni, and more. Each of the stands flew a rainbow flag. The longest lineup was for a white truck with an open side called Big Johnson's Lollies. People walked away licking rainbow frozen treats.

Fatima said, "Let's skip the popsicles."

Garrett turned to Sam and Riley. "Where do we go for the best food?"

Sam smiled. Riley looked at his partner. "Milo's?"

Sam nodded, looking at Fatima's feet. "It's on the other side, you want to change first?"

Fatima lifted the hem of her dress, revealing red running shoes. "I'm good."

They followed Sam and Riley past people licking lollies and posing for selfies.

Riley put his hand on Sam's shoulder. "So far, so good."

They passed a clutch of young people. A couple of them wore cowboy hats. One of the others wore a Spiderman outfit.

"Hi Garrett and Fatima!"

They turned, seeing Sanjiv with a man who was her height with black hair and smiling blue eyes. "The wedding was beautiful." She touched Fatima's arm. "You look stunning."

Fatima smiled. "Thank you. How are you feeling?"

Sanjiv patted her stomach. "Much better." She pointed at the man with her. "This is Ben."

Ben and Garrett shook hands. Ben smiled. "Thanks for the business." He winked. "Now we can afford diapers."

Fatima laughed. "Now we can afford a honeymoon!"

Garrett nodded at his cousin. "This is my cousin Riley and his partner Sam."

Sanjiv smiled. "We've already met."

Fatima squinted as she looked from Riley and Sam, to Sanjiv and Ben, and back again. "What's the story?"

Riley looked around to see if anyone was nearby. "Sanjiv came and met with us–" He pointed at Sam. "–and Gwen, Jean, and Sydney."

Garrett looked at Sanjiv, "And?"

Sanjiv smiled. "I wanted to see the whole picture, and it

turned out by working together we were able to coordinate our strategies." She looked at Ella who smiled with recognition. Sanjiv leaned down and picked up Ella who hugged her around the neck with one arm, licking the lolly with the other. Sanjiv said, "This is Ben."

Ella nodded, pointing the lolly Sanjiv's belly. "You put the baby in there?"

Ben opened his mouth, looking at Sanjiv who smiled at Ella. "Yes, he did."

Ella smiled. "Good job."

. . . .

An hour later, Fatima tucked her arm around Garrett's elbow while they enjoyed a moment alone in the crowd. They turned to see a woman with short platinum blonde hair and blue eyes. She wore a neon blue jacket and magenta high-heeled cowboy boots. She talked into her cell phone while nibbling one of Milo's creations.

Sam leaned in on the other side of Garrett. "That's Miriam Webley, the food critic. Dressed like that–with all the queens at the festival–she travels incognito." He handed plates to Fatima and Garrett. "Enjoy."

Fatima looked at the burger with its whole-wheat bun, layers of cheese, bacon, and tomato. She picked it up, bit in, closing her eyes.

Garrett took his elk salami sub in two hands, looked at the layers of meat, tomatoes, lettuce, cheese, and pickles. He took a bite from the end, looked at Sam then said, "This is amazing. This and Starlight's buffalo ribs are to die for."

Sam nodded. "Those two are favourites at markets for miles around."

"Here you go." Riley set a glass of red wine in front of Fatima, handing a latte to Garrett.

Fatima sipped the wine from the plastic goblet. "You're a

darling. Wasn't it a Starlight who won the barrel racing?"

Riley sat down next to Sam. "Yep and Rollie, the welder from Corporation, won the fastest time for putting underwear on a goat."

Fatima polished off the last bite of her burger, touching Sam's hand. "Okay if we borrow your truck so we can go back to the farm and get changed?"

"Of course." He leaned over, reaching into his pants pocket, handing her the keys, winking at Fatima. She blushed, glancing at Garrett.

Siobhan and Dayna came to sit at the table. Dayna said, "Okay if we go back to the farm to get changed?"

Garrett lifted an eyebrow at Fatima who didn't look back at him. She said, "Sure," holding up the keys.

Jacolynne and Ella arrived next. Jac put her hand on Fatima's shoulder. "Would you mind if I changed out of this dress? It's kinda hot in here."

Sam laughed.

Jac and Dayna asked, "What's so funny?"

Garrett wiped his mouth with a paper napkin, shaking his head. He stood up, grabbing his latte with one hand, and Fatima's hand with the other. "Shall we go?"

· · · · · · · · · · · · · · ·

YYC News
BREAKING NEWS

Approximately twenty uniformed officers of the Calgary Police Services Tactical Unit descended upon a home in the Altadore district at noon today. Members of the Calgary chapter of the Hells Angels frequent the property.

CPS Organized Crime Inspector Karl Frederick said, "Several members of the Hells Angels were arrested at the scene. A cache of weapons and drugs were seized along with several laptop computers."

· · · · · · · · · · · · · · ·

"What's happening over there?" Jac leaned forward from the rear seat of Sam's Ford pickup truck. They'd just returned to Corporation after changing into casual clothes at the farm. She pointed at the gooseneck trailer under the pink fifty-foot sausage. A crowd of onlookers gathered around the trailer. Red, blue, and white lights flashed from both the RCMP vehicles and a red fire engine. One man sat half way up the shaft, stradling the sculpture.

Garrett squinted at the black haired man wearing a white shirt and blue jeans. He looked to be close to three hundred pounds and kept leaning back, pulling at something with his right hand.

David asked, "Is he doing what I think he's doing?"

Garrett stopped the truck about thirty metres from the edge of the crowd. "I think it's Giles Patriot."

Fatima opened her door. "That asshole?"

David sat in the back seat. "You're right dad, it is him."

Mark slid out his door, reaching for Ella. "I hope we haven't missed all the fun."

Garrett pocketed the keys, waiting while everyone piled out. He followed behind Dayna and Siobhan who had changed into shorts and T-shirts. They walked up to the edge of the crowd. A man with a ball cap and a red quad pulled a white freezer on a trailer. He pulled up behind them. "Dicksicles! Get you're big Dicksicles!"

Ella looked, saying something into her dad's ear. Mark reached into his pants pocket with a free hand, pulling out a twenty. "Jac, you want one?"

Jac shook her head. "I don't think so."

Mark waved the bill at the Dicksicle man, buying a lolly for Ella. Others in the crowd saw the cool treat, and a lineup formed.

"I want my sign back!" Giles Patriot wore alligator skin boots. He spoke over the crowd, hoisting a yellow chainsaw. "I'm gonna Bobbittize this sausage if I don't get my face back!"

"Guess his stint at rehab was cut short." Garrett turned his shoulders to one side, easing his way through the crowd. Fatima took his hand, following. They eventually broke through to stand about four metres from the goose-neck trailer and the paper mache and wood sculpture. Sydney and Sutherland managed to move the crowd back about five metres from the trailer.

Riley balanced on the framework at the neck of the trailer. He said, "Come on down off of there before you fall and break something."

One of Giles' supporters–a drinking buddy–wore a black cowboy hat. He climbed onto the trailer, waving a beer at the crowd. "He's got a right to get back what's his."

Sydney pointed at the cowboy. "You! Freddy! Get down from there."

Freddy ignored her. Sydney reached up, grabbing the back of his belt, yanking him off the trailer. A pair of drag queens steadied him. Freddy looked over his shoulder, shrugged them off, and took a step back toward the trailer. Sydney put the flat of her right hand against Freddy's chest. He swung with his right fist. Sydney ducked, turning him around. She kicked the feet out from under him.

A calf roper threw her arms in the air. "Time!"

A woman next to the calf roper said, "Freddy! Don't you

know what happens to people who mess with Sydney?"

Patriot pulled on the chainsaw's starter rope. The engine sputtered and died.

Riley pointed at Patriot. "If you cut there, you might touch off the fuse." He looked at Sydney. "Better move the crowd away." He waved his hands at the people near the head of the fifty-foot sausage. "It's loaded."

Garrett looked at Fatima who had her hand over her mouth. She asked, "Did he say what I think he said?"

"Loaded with what?" Jac asked.

Sam said, "Fireworks. Riley was going to set it off tonight."

Patriot yanked on the chainsaw's cord. It sputtered.

David turned to Jac. "This is getting way too crazy."

Four cowboys rolled up a hay bail. One reached into his pants pocket and pulled out a knife to cut the twine. Then they rolled the bail open. Riley asked, "Good idea. Can you guys open another bail on the other side so he doesn't break his neck when he falls?"

"Ella!" Jac caused a lull in the crowd noise.

Garrett looked to his right. Ella had her shorts and big girl panties around her knees. Her hands were around her ankles with her round backside pointed at the sun.

Mark asked, "Ella? What are you doing?"

Ella said, "Charging my vagina!"

Mark looked at Jac who had her hand covering her mouth. "Why?"

"Becaue I'm Rainbow Blaster and I have super powers!" Ella straightened. Jac pulled up her shorts. Ella raised her right hand. "I shoot rainbows from my fingers."

Patriot pulled on the cord. The two-cycle engine crackled to life at the same time the crowd began to laugh. Patriot found himself in the middle of a cloud of blue exhaust. He swung the chainsaw down and to his left, missing the toe of his boot by millimetres. The engine growled, the saw ripping into paper mache and wood. Riley waved the crowd back. Sydney and the constable opened their arms, walking toward the crowd. Sawdust and bits of pink paper peppered Patriot arms. He gripped the shaft with his knees.

Garrett could smell chainsaw exhaust, burnt wood, and something else.

Riley waved his arms, yelling. "A fuse is lit! Back up!"

Garrett looked to the left. The crowd was twenty metres away and retreating. Fatima grabbed his elbow. Jac carried Ella back from the trailer, Mark following. Sydney waved her arms above her head. "Get back!"

Patriot leaned back. The chainsaw chewed through the far side. His mouth formed an **O**. His face paled. His eyes rolled back to white. The chainsaw fell to the left side, bouncing on the ground, the engine dying. Patriot rolled to the left, slid off the sausage, missing the edge of the trailer, and flopping onto the hay. He lay there on his back, arms out wide. The toe of his left boot pointed at the sky. The toe of the right boot was ripped off, a bloody mess of bone and flesh.

In the momentary silence, Sydney waved at the ambulance. "Man down! We need an EMT!"

In less than a minute, a woman in navy blue jump suit was kneeling next to Patriot. She opened a red plastic toolbox with her purple-gloved hands. Sydney knelt next to her. The EMT cut the boot away from the foot. She had just freed the remains of the foot when the first of the aerial repeater fireworks went FOOMP!

A shell launched from the tip of the sausage. It trailed a white tail of burning gas. The shell exploded overtop a hay bail next to the corral. A shower of heat and light spilled to the ground. Another shell fired from the tip followed by more. Garrett grabbed one of Patriot's arms. Fatima grabbed the other. The EMT grabbed both his legs. Sydney hefted the first aid gear. They carried Patriot about thirty metres from the exploding shaft. Flames began to lick the sculpture. It split, forming a V. More shells fired into blue. White smoke rose up from the hay bails.

A siren wailed, followed by another.

Garrett and Fatima stood back while the EMT wrapped a dressing around Patriot's foot and ankle.

Sydney said, "Get him in the ambulance." She looked back at the sausage. It was still firing shells of red, white, and purple. A grey cloud of smoke created a canvas for the exploding colours. The town's volunteer firemen had to choose one fire so they chose the hay bales next to the corral. They aimed their hoses at the white smoke boiling up from the burning bales even as more fireworks erupted from the tip of the sausage. The smoke cloud rose and spread. A rainbow of colours brushed against the smoke.

Garrett looked for his kids. David, Dayna, and Siobhan stood behind Ella who sat on her father's shoulders. Her right index finger pointed at the rainbow. For a moment she was silhouetted in front of the arc painted across the smoke. A fusilade of exploding fireworks splashed more colours onto the grey backdrop. Ella's fingers fanned, touching the multicoloured arc.

Garrett watched as Riley tapped Sydney on the shoulder. Riley said, "The sculpture was designed to burn. It was supposed to be set up in the centre of the corral, not out here."

Sydney nodded. "Our friend had other ideas. And it doesn't look like anyone else is hurt."

Riley looked at Patriot. "Is he gonna be okay?"

Sydney shrugged. "He'll have to learn to walk again."

There was another explosion from the fifty-foot sausage. Sydney asked, "Is that the last one?"

Riley shook his head. "Nope."

Sydney shook her head. "You gotta be shittin' me."

Jean rolled up in a borrowed green Ford pickup. Cathy sat

in the passenger seat. Both women climbed out. Jean asked, "What happened?"

Riley pointed at the smoking sculpture.

Sam said, "All our planning and this happens."

Cathy looked at the broken shaft with smoke pouring from its tip. "Where are Patriot's signs?"

Sam opened his hands. "We stacked them face down on the bottom of the trailer under the sculpture."

Fatima smiled. "You mean Patriot was sitting on top them the whole time?"

Jean looked at the trailer. "Where did the trailer come from?"

Riley looked around to see who was within earshot. "We borrowed it from the Richardson acreage."

Jean looked at the fire truck and crew as they sprayed water on the smouldering hay bails. "We were going to have a bonfire anyway."

Cathy moved to the back of the green pickup, dropping the tailgate. She slid out a couple of green street signs. Garrett read RICHARDSON ROAD on one of them. She carried them toward the trailer, tossing the signs under the sculpture.

Garrett walked over to the truck, grabbing a couple of the green signs. He recognized the look of determined rage on Cathy Gartner's face as he handed her the signs. To his left he saw Jean on the phone. "We have to move fast. The bonfire is happening now. Tell them to bring the stuff."

A minute later, the sculpture and trailer were engulfed in flame. The wooden base of the trailer was smouldering; the tires were acrid rings of flame. The ambulance passed through the smoke. Its lights flashed as it headed for the hospital. A steady stream of pickups and cars began to arrive. Trunks opened, tailgates dropped. Some people carried red Rod for Mayor T-shirts, tossing them into the fire. Others carried lawn signs saying, In Rod We Trust and Richardson 4 Mayor. They were thrown onto the flames. Boxes of papers were thrown on top of the flaming hay next to the trailer.

A pickup truck backed up near the fire. Two men climbed out of the truck and into the box. They hefted a wooden statue up onto its feet. The crowd roared.

Riley looked at Garrett. "Richardson came back from BC with a statue of himself. He had it mounted on a platform near the lake."

The men in the back of the truck set the statue on the edge of the tailgate.

Riley said, "One!"

Jean said, "Two!"

Cathy said, "Burn the asshole!"

The men flipped the statue. It landed head first, toppling onto the hay.

Another truck backed up to the bonfire. The driver opened the door, swinging himself into the truck box. He began to lift and throw broken wooden pallets onto the pile. He finished by tossing a pair of A frame Nova Bank signs into the flames. Ten minutes later, the sculpture had collapsed. People in the crowd marked the event by throwing beer cans, coffee cups, and Rod bobblehead dolls into the fire. Garrett looked around him. Riley had his arm around Sam's shoulder. Siobhan and Dayna held hands.

Fatima leaned her head against Garrett's shoulder. "Who could ask for a better wedding?"

Jac kissed her daughter on the cheek. David watched his niece. Garrett recognized the longing in his son's eyes.

THIRTY-NINE

Wednesday, July 2

0

Small Town Sausage Lives Up to the Hype

by Miriam Webley
– Food Columnist

Corporation, Alberta put on its First Annual Sausage Festival yesterday. As a freelance food critic, yours truly was at the event with the aim of sampling Corporation's claim to fame, the inimitable sausage. Corporation lived up to its reputation in expected and unexpected ways.

As part of the celebrations, Corporation staged fireworks emitting from a fifty-foot pink sausage sculpture. Someone should have told the planners that fireworks are a dish best served after dark. Four o'clock in the afternoon is hardly a suitable time for such an event. The poor planning resulted in two fires. One involved a pair of unlucky hay bales. That blaze was extinguished by a hapless small town fire department, fine representatives of the town's shallow gene pool.

The other fire led to a pseudo anarchistic bonfire where frolicking locals burned trash, a wooden effigy of former Mayor Rodney Richardson, and other detritus.

One pleasant surprise was that some of the visitors

have exquisite taste. This reporter estimates twenty-five aristocratic women attended the event. They must have been expecting a far grander spectacle because they were decked in elaborate ball gowns.

Another revelation was the delightful flavours created by carnivorous amateur chefs. All manner of pork, beef, and wild meat dishes were prepared by a variety of vendors. A food truck overseen by Chef Milo produced some remarkably acceptable cre-ations. This reporter was pleasantly enthused by the presentation, the overall delectability of the ingredients, and the choice of pleasing accoutrements. It must be said the reaction from clients of Milo's creations ranged from ecstatic to blissful. Even if manners were more along the lines of abysmal and atrocious.

A bit of advice to organizers: Porta Potties do not inspire foodie confidence where food is prepared.

The food at this event is granted a Webley four stars out of five.

· · · · · · · · · · · · · · ·

YYC News

Radio Host Arrested

Radio personality Giles Patriot has been placed under arrest. RCMP Constable Colleen Turner of the Red Deer detachment said, "When he is released from Red Deer hospital, he will be transported to Calgary, and formally charged."

Patriot's predicament follows a series of arrests connected to a drug cartel operating in Corporation, Alberta, and Port Warwick, Ontario. Billionaires Kristopher and Harold Krotch were also arrested. Six members of the Hells Angels were arrested in Calgary during a coordinated operation involving members of the RCMP and the Calgary Police Service.

CPS Organized Crime Inspector Karl Frederick said, "Information on the names of the accused, and their individual charges will be announced on Friday. This investigation involves the RCMP, the OPP, and the Calgary Police Service." On May twelfth of this year, eight men, including one RCMP constable, were killed at Mayor Richardson's acreage near Corporation, Alberta. A second RCMP constable arrived at the scene and was wounded by the mayor during a gun battle. Today Frederick said,

"The CPS, OPP, and RCMP continue to investigate links between the Corporation massacre and business operations associated with Nova Bank."

Jean Nesbitt who is Corporation's secretarty and interim mayor said, "Patriot's arrest means the last of Rod and his gang have left our town. Now we can finish the work of healing."

FORTY

<u>Friday, July 4</u>

O

So this is what an after wedding banquet looks like?" David smiled, looking around the house. It was located in Calgary's Bridgeland district and converted into a restaurant. Six tables rubbed shoulders in the front half. They were using three tables placed side by side to accommodate the eight of them, taking up more than a third of the space. The outside deck was empty. It was Garrett's idea to get the family together for a dinner in Calgary's Little Italy to put a final candle on their celebrations.

Waitress Martika was thirty-five, wore jeans, a white blouse, and a wry smile. She set the first pizza, ham and pineapple, down in the middle of the table. "Back in a minute."

Garrett said, "Thank you."

Mark was the first to dive in. He cut the melted cheese on one slice to set in front of Ella. Jac held Ella's hands to keep them safe from the heat. Ella leaned closer, sniffing the ham and pineapple. She turned her head to look at her mother. "Hot?"

Jac nodded. Mark reached over to cut the slice into slivers, picking up the plate to blow and cool.

Dayna handed out slices. Fatima leaned close to Garrett,

hugging his arm.

His phone rang as Siobhan set a plate and a slice in front of him. "Thanks." He reached for the phone, reading the name. He looked at Fatima. "It's Riley."

Fatima shrugged. "Better answer it."

He put the phone on speaker. "What's up?"

Riley sounded breathless. "Sam said I'd better call you."

The tension in Riley's voice put a halt to the sounds of mastication. Eyes focused on Garrett.

Ella said, "Riley!"

He said, "Hey Ella." His volume decreased. "I just phoned to warn you. Luke put a video on YouTube before checking with us."

David took a bite of pizza, raising his eyebrows.

Garrett looked out the sliding glass doors to the deck. "Okay."

Riley said, "It's titled Garrett the Carrot and the Burning Sausage."

Jac laughed out loud, looking at Ella who asked, "Is it cool now?"

Martika arrived with another pizza. She looked at Garrett. "I thought you looked familiar."

Riley said, "The video is setting records on YouTube. It's at over half a million views."

Garrett's chin dropped.

Riley said, "There's only one shot of you, the rest is of Patriot, the crowd, the fireworks, the fires, the wands, and Ella pointing at the rainbow."

Martika set the second pizza next to the first. "You're a hero around here. Everyone knows the Krotch brothers are connected to La Familia and the Hells Angels. A month ago a couple of Angels came in here to threaten us and offer protection. You shut them down." She looked over her shoulder. "Hey Peter!" The swinging door to the kitchen opened revealing a man wearing a white T-shirt and three days growth of beard. She pointed. "It's Garrett the Carrot!"

Peter wiped his hands on a white apron, walking over to the table, offering his hand to Garrett. They shook and Peter asked, "How's the pizza?"

David raised goal post hands. "Fantastic as always."

Garrett smiled. "It's our favourite."

Martika pointed at Garrett and Fatima. "They got married" She blushed. "Sorry, I was eavesdropping."

Peter asked, "You like chocolate cheese cake?"

They all heard Riley's voice on speaker. "So you're not mad about the video?"

Ella asked, "Chocolate?"

Peter smiled at her. "On the house for you!"

Ella's eyes sparkled blue, watching her grandfather.

Jac said, "We'll be pretty full after all this pizza."

Garrett sensed what might be coming and leaned back, watching his granddaughter.

Ella pointed at her mother. "Are you shittin' me? He said chocolate."

<u>Acknowledgments</u>

Thank you doctors Bruce and Navaid.

Thanks to the late Wayne Gunn.

Thank you Richard for the invaluable coffee shop advice, insights and openness to this new venture. Jeremy, thank you for making the book so much better with your edits. Celia, your input is the icing on this particular cake.

Thanks to Pages, Owl's Nest, Shelf Life, and all independent booksellers and supporters of Calgary writers.

Thanks to web designer Stephen.
www.garryryan.ca

Thanks to creative writers at Nickle, Bowness, Lord Beaverbrook, Alternative, Forest Lawn, and Queen Elizabeth.

Sharon, Karma, Ben,
Luke, Indiana, and Ella.
Here we go again.

Garry Ryan has published 12 books of fiction. He is a winner of the Lambda Literary Prize and has been selected for Calgary's Freedom of Expression Award. He drinks mochas and lives in Calgary.